Short Blasts

An eclectic mix of short stories from the pen of Mai Griffin (including Young Echoes – a short stand-alone prequel to the Ghostly Echoes Series)

Also by Mai Griffin

Ghostly Echoes
A Poisonous Echo
Dangerous Echoes
Haunting Echoes
Restless Echoes

Somebody Came

All Rights Reserved

First published in Great Britain in 2020 by U P Publications
Registered Office: St George's House, George Street,
Huntingdon, Cambridgeshire, UK PE29 3GH

Cover design copyright © U P Publications 2020

A CIP Catalogue record of this book is available from the British Library

This edition ISBN 978-1-912777-41-9
eBook ISBN 978-1-912777-42-6

FIRST PAPERBACK EDITION

Published by U P Publications

www.uppbooks.com
www.maiwriting.com
www.maigriffin.com

Short Blasts

_____

Mai Griffin

U P PUBLICATIONS
2020

Contents

Change of Heart

Delia sat on the edge of her elegant brass bed gathering strength to face the day. The familiar aura of depression threatened to envelop her again. Being mindful of her many blessings never helped her to face the day. She felt drained. Even sitting up was an effort, yet the doctor assured her that there was nothing wrong with her; in fact, for sixty-plus, she was amazingly fit. Delia knew better – there had always been something wrong with her heart. It apparently did a reasonable job pumping, but it had misled her badly more than once.

Before her fifteenth birthday, she almost ran away with her boyfriend although her head told her that he was no good. He proved it by taking her friend instead, while Delia was under house arrest. She'd narrowly missed being ruined, as they used to say in those days.

Her heart recovered enough to let her down so often before she met Derek that, when it yearned to accept his proposal, she didn't trust it at all.

Disillusioned, he went to Malaya to fight in what wasn't even called a war. The long, bloody mess of battles euphemistically labelled 'The Emergency', took many lives, including his. Delia imagined him fighting – with fierce abandon – feeling that he had nothing to live for and, consumed by guilt, she lost interest in her own future.

In her mid-twenties she'd married dark, handsome Robert. Now, grey and balding, he was planning a small party to celebrate their ruby anniversary and Delia's treacherous heart went out to him. She'd been honest from the beginning, admitting only a fondness for him. His claim that he had love enough for them both had proved true, over the years. His eagerness to please and mild acceptance of her irrational bad temper inevitably increased her anguish. She knew how totally unreasonable she was and, at such times, came close to loving him, if pity was akin to love.

Today, at Robert's insistence, she must shop for a new dress. "You spend so little on yourself, dear," he said, putting his arm round her as she prepared to leave. "If you really like something, don't look at the price ticket …we don't have to economise." He always urged her not to worry about money, but he also knew that she was careful and wouldn't take advantage.

Attempting to sound enthusiastic, Delia smoothed her greying hair away from her lightly rouged face and assured him that she had her bankcard and would enjoy a buying spree. His obvious pleasure justified the lie. She used make-up only to please him and had little interest in fashion. Fortunately, her figure was still trim and an envious friend once said that she could wear anything – even a flour sack.

Thanks to Robert, she had no problem finding jewellery to dress up plain outfits. He liked to surprise her with little gifts, even when it wasn't her birthday or Christmas, and had a surprisingly reliable eye for pieces that didn't need to be expensive to look good.

In return, she'd been a dutiful wife in every sense and even this fed her guilt. Robert deserved more. She would have been able to give her heart and mind totally to Derek …how she'd loved him! If only he'd known, he'd have been more careful of his safety. He would have returned to her and a life of happy fulfilment.

The short stroll from their sea-front apartment to the shops was her only exercise so, by habit, Delia refused a lift. Robert, anxious that she shouldn't overtire herself, always met her on the promenade for coffee before driving her home for lunch. As she walked, she made up her mind to enjoy the coming celebration and considered what colour she might wear, burgundy perhaps, to match the anniversary, or green because it was Robert's favourite colour.

Derek's favourite colour was blue. It became hers too because it matched his eyes and he looked so good in it. Oh, why had she allowed her thoughts to return to him? Daydreams of what might have been had surfaced much more often during the last few years – perhaps because she felt cheated as she left middle-age behind. With renewed determination, Delia gritted her teeth, gave herself a mental shake and headed for the shopping centre.

Two hours later, satisfied that on dress, shoes and handbag, she'd spent enough to satisfy Robert, she walked along the sea front to the café. Ribbons of white froth sparkled at the edge of the incoming tide, washing clean the dingy accumulation of litter collecting in heaps along the breakers. It was windy and, despite the April sunshine, not a warm day. The promenade's few pedestrians were moving briskly, so her eyes were drawn inevitably to the golden-haired man on the stone bench. His profile seemed familiar. She hesitated – then drew a quick breath. Her throat constricted. Blood pounded in her ears, deafening her to the crashing waves. Derek! It was Derek. Rationale deserted her as she rushed impetuously to reach him, but when she was only a few feet away – to her profound embarrassment – he turned to look directly at her. His smile increased her confusion …even his clear sapphire eyes could have been Derek's but now she saw that he wasn't a young man. It was merely the sun's bright halo, which had turned his grey hair to a youthful blonde. Was she going mad?

She'd inadvertently come far too close to avoid speaking. "I do beg your pardon. Please excuse me," she gasped, "I mistook you for someone else."

"No problem," he said, standing and indicating that she should join him. "Do sit for a moment, you seem distressed."

It would have been churlish to refuse so Delia propped her parcels at her feet and took a deep breath. His look of concern was enough, without words, to put her at ease and she felt no awkwardness in sharing his seat. She was more put out by the pointing finger of a child whose family had been heading for the same bench. They stood nearby as if waiting for her to leave which, perversely, made her hold her ground.

Turning her back to them, Delia apologised again and explained that he reminded her of a dearly loved friend who had been killed in Malaya in 1950.

"Ah, yes, many died in the Emergency," he nodded adding, to her astonishment, "I was there."

The immediate thought that he might have met Derek was voiced before she could dismiss it as ridiculous and when he replied, "Yes, it is possible," Delia's senses swam. Her stomach churned and had she not been seated her legs would have given way. He touched her hand gently and said, "I understand my dear ...you've carried a load of guilt because you survived and still feel bitter because you had to face the future without him." His empathy was too much of a shock and she burst into tears. The obnoxious child was enjoying Delia's distress from a few feet away, but the girl's parents summoned her and the family moved away.

Alone with the stranger now, his intense, sympathetic gaze encouraged her and Delia unburdened herself of her regrets. "Were you married or engaged?" she asked. "If the engagement had been broken off, would you have taken more risks as you fought?"

The man, about her own age she guessed, stared into the distance. His kindly eyes clouded as he recalled and tried to describe the heat and humidity of the jungle – birdsong reverberating in the still air – wild creatures calling to each other and their instant ominous silence when an unseen presence alarmed them.

"We were under canvas when we were lucky," he said. "Washing in leech-infested rivers – despite the snakes, monitor lizards and the odd crocodile – was a rare treat, otherwise we stayed dirty. Touching the leeches with a lighted cigarette soon made them loosen their grip," he grinned boyishly, "and banging our boots before putting them on, to tip out lurking scorpions, became second nature." When Delia's hand flew to her mouth in horror, he looked contrite and touched her cheek lightly to stem her tears. "It was a long time ago and the hardships were easier to bear than the constant fear of attack. We knew that the enemy, in territory familiar to them, could be within yards of our camp, watching us night and day. When we did have to go into action it was almost a relief and every skirmish we won brought the end nearer, or so we hoped."

Shrugging one shoulder, a gesture vaguely familiar to her, he said sadly, "We felt that nobody in Europe, at the time, wanted to know about the fighting, and now it's all forgotten."

"But *I* followed the news – *I* cared," Delia insisted. "I was such a fool not to realise how much I loved Derek until I had to go on existing without him. If only he'd known …if only I'd promised to wait for him – things might have been different."

"Believe me, he was probably quite confident that you'd marry him eventually. Your turning him down was merely a minor setback. I guarantee he carried your photograph with him everywhere and always boasted that you were his girl, knowing what was in your heart better than you did yourself."

"If only I could believe that he didn't die feeling rejected, it would be such a relief." Delia found a dry place on her handkerchief and dabbed her eyes, trying to smile when the man assured her that he'd never met a man who gave up trying to change a girl's mind after only one rejection!

"Believe me," he said. "I'm speaking from experience. I lost my best girl too, just before going overseas, but had every intention of finding her again. Forgive yourself and make the most of life. That's what he would have wanted." He stood and was walking away before Delia could recover sufficiently to ask his name or where she might contact him again. As if reading her thoughts, he turned, gave her a smart salute and called, "Put the past behind you ...be happy."

Gathering up her parcels Delia hastened to catch him, but the esplanade had become more crowded as people left the beach and surged towards the restaurants for lunch. He was nowhere to be seen but her frustration dissipated within seconds ...it didn't matter. His words had comforted her immeasurably – what more could he have added? For years, she'd been incredibly foolish, dwelling on those last moments with Derek. She was suddenly sure that he wouldn't have accepted her rejection meekly, he would have tried again, and the knowledge released her from self-reproach. Her weariness evaporated.

The breeze seemed warmer and as she approached the restaurant, each step became lighter.

When she saw Robert, she felt intensely proud of him. He stood to greet her and she laughed aloud at his look of astonishment when she kissed his cheek. Feeling the need to explain her unusual conduct, Delia assured him cheerfully, "I've had an absolutely wonderful morning. I hope you'll like what I've bought."

As she opened her shopping bags for him to peep inside, Delia noted with a slight frown that the rude child she'd tried to ignore earlier was also in the restaurant, sitting nearby and still staring at her. Fortunately, the family was too far away for her to hear the child whisper, "Look mummy, there's that funny lady we saw near the beach – the one who was crying and talking to herself!"

Robert sensed the change in Delia's demeanour and, without understanding, happily accepted her good mood. He had no way of knowing that he was now the only man in her life and, for the first time ever, when she touched his hand, her heart was full of love.

Bar Fly

For a moment, her eyes abandoned the street beyond the bright entrance to the bar and looked down, with satisfaction, at her shapely knees. She was quite sure that many younger women would envy them. The low lighting where she sat was kind, but it didn't matter, she always took care with her make-up; at her age, the skin could become dry, making the inevitable lines more difficult to conceal. Tonight, she felt especially good. Her expensive new foundation made her look half her forty-nine years!

She became aware that the old man at the other end of the bar was eyeing her again; she adjusted her skirt primly, flushing with annoyance. She was no cheap tart, like the floozy who'd enticed her first husband away. She'd married again, happily, but was widowed within five years.

No other man had attracted her until a few weeks ago when Peter walked into the bar and their eyes met. She felt faint – he was so like her late husband. His look was intense; he was obviously attracted to her. Realising that he came here regularly, after work, she abandoned the other haunts she'd used to spread her custom and to avoid being labelled a barfly or a lush!

He came later than his friends and it was their usual greeting, 'Hi Pete', which gave her his name.

Once, when he'd been the first to arrive, she'd sensed his desire to speak with her, before the others joined him, but there was little time. His overture had been hesitant; gentlemanly: endearingly shy. Without approaching, he said, "Good evening. May I buy you a drink?", and, as she smilingly accepted, the others entered ending any further exchange. They frequently smiled at each other unobserved: secret, stolen moments.

Without being obvious, he contrived to include her when ordering a round; she always acknowledged his gesture, raising her glass to him before sipping slowly, relishing the fact that he knew her favourite cocktail and wanted to please her. It amused her that he always averted his eyes, not letting his companions suspect their growing intimacy. Planning the life they might share, filled her dreams and waking hours. It didn't matter that he was younger; if he didn't care why should she? She was, however, surprised, as the weeks passed, that he did not make a more determined attempt to speak.

It worried her.

She was embarrassed to be seen in the bar every evening. The barman was becoming familiar – in a friendly way of course, nothing unseemly, but she was offended by the constant ogling of the old man who had also started coming more often. Deirdre Miller was a respectable woman. Not only had she ignored Women's Lib, but she'd been totally unimpressed by the whole furore around the sexual revolution …all that was for other people; those with loose morals and no self-esteem.

Deirdre had to face the fact that her behaviour could be misinterpreted, so she deliberately avoided the man's stare, pointing her neatly crossed knees away from him as she swung on the high stool.

Driven to extreme measures, she'd followed Peter a week ago and all became clear. Outside the subway station, to her chagrin, he met another woman! Deirdre's long nails hurt her palms as she clenched her hands in dismay – his reluctance to advance their relationship was explained. He was married!

Naturally, being honourable, he had subdued his own desires to avoid hurting his wife. Unable to tear herself away she followed them, observing their every gesture. They did not link arms or even touch hands. They actually appeared cool with each other. Reaching the barrier, the woman glanced back, revealing her face. It was pale and plain. Her small mouth, devoid of lipstick, was almost lost in the shadow of an over-large nose; her eyes were invisible behind thick glasses.

Since then she'd detected an air of sadness about Peter. Being so handsome, he must hate being tied to such a wife when, with her, he could be so happy ...if only!

Accepting that he would not speak to her, did not stop her from being impatient for a sight of Peter. Trembling slightly, she remembered the disconcerting feeling that the woman had looked directly at her, as if she'd sensed they were being followed. She ordered another Martini and sipped it slowly. Having missed lunch in order to have her special hairdo and choose new cosmetics she realised that the drink was having more effect on her than usual. Coming out of her reverie Deirdre eyed her glass suspiciously – it was almost full; how could that be?

The arrival of the now familiar group interrupted her thoughts. Peter followed immediately as though he had waited for them to precede him, not trusting himself alone with her. Poor man, how he must be suffering!

Again, a drink arrived for her and as she lifted it towards him, he averted his eyes instantly. Before he turned away, she saw anguish crease his handsome face and the effect on Deirdre was immediate; all her protective instincts surfaced. She could not bear to picture his miserable home life; his few hours here were probably his only relief.

More than a little light-headed, wild thoughts raced unbidden through her mind.

She had to rescue him; an unfortunate accident at the tube station would take care of his wife! It would be simple... a quick shove and a rapid retreat, unobserved, in the throng of people pressing forward for a vicarious thrill, eager to see the source of the screams! Even if the woman didn't meet him tonight, there would be other nights. Deirdre didn't care how many times she had to follow him to rescue him from his misery. In her hazy, heady state, she had few misgivings; she was doing the right thing for Peter. He would never know he owed her his freedom, but it wasn't his gratitude she wanted. She was not doing it for her own gain although she fervently hoped he would turn to her for the loving care she longed to give him.

At last the group seemed to be breaking up; she must leave before them, to wait out of sight – following should be easy on the crowded streets. She almost fell off the barstool in her panic but was saved by a man's arm. Deirdre looked up into the face she had come to loathe – the regular who leered at her every night. Over his head she saw that Peter had noticed the incident. It was so embarrassing; she couldn't get away quickly enough. With a curt nod of thanks, she pulled away from her rescuer, cutting off his attempts to detain and speak to her. Now, she thought as she walked out, he will think he has a right to attach himself to me …it was infuriating! Why couldn't it have been other arms that caught me? Peter seemed surprised to see her go, and she paused in the lobby wondering if he would follow her; perhaps she should have tried this strategy before! He did not, but if she had harboured any doubts about his interest they would have been banished entirely by that precious glance. When his eyes met hers, she read a longing that matched her own.

Soon – sooner than he dreamed – they could be together always.

Outside, the air was uncomfortably cool; fortunately, Peter soon came out and strode off purposefully. She followed, concealed by the crowds. To her satisfaction the woman was at the station, waiting in the same place as before. Annoyance, as she pointed to her watch, made her features even more unattractive. When they crossed the barrier, Deirdre bought a ticket and followed them to the platform, only vaguely aware that she was not her normal self. She felt terribly sick and her taut nerves anticipated the moment when she would send his wife to eternity.

A train was due within seconds.

The engine suddenly loomed in the mouth of the tunnel – she was at the woman's shoulder, hands raised, poised in readiness, when Peter spoke. Above the roar he shouted, "Never mind Sis, we'll go tomorrow!"

Her arms fell limply to her sides as the train hissed to a standstill. She'd come close to a pointless murder; she had nothing to fear from his sister! Thank God she'd found out in time!

Her eyes closed in horror and the train was pulling away before she realised, they were still waiting. When they began conversing again, curiosity froze her to the spot. Although it was difficult to hear everything, she was sure they were discussing her. She heard the words, *"Female – blonde – every night – bar,"* and edged nearer. The woman laughed.

"You should never have bought her a drink. What a stupid way to spend your hard-earned money!"

"Don't be miserable, I only did it once," Peter replied.

Another train was approaching so he raised his voice, "She's just a pathetic creature who has seen better days. Anyway..." The engine thundered towards them out of the arch, but she caught his words clearly; ..."I was alone and couldn't stand the obvious way she kept staring at me. The drink distracted her!"

The train's roar merged with the pounding in her brain as she staggered towards the edge of the platform, wishing only to end her humiliation.

A hand caught her arm and she whirled to see the man from the bar.

The shock sobered her instantly!

Where was she?

What had she been about to do?

Dazed with relief and surprise, she took in his words and appearance.

His wavy grey hair was windswept, but he wasn't as old as she'd first thought. His intense blue eyes looked earnest, so her mortification was increased when she focussed on his words. "Please don't go! It has taken me weeks to pluck up the courage to speak. Will you join me for dinner? I'd like the chance to meet you properly, instead of just sharing the odd drink from afar!"

The Birthday Present

Waiting for dawn, Terry's confidence ebbed. This place, the Spanish village where her mother had once lived, was no longer tiny. Now a mixture of ancient and modern, it had melded with other communities. Here in its heart, where her hopes had been pinned, the narrow streets were a bewildering maze that would daunt any stranger. The likelihood of finding an elderly resident who might recognise Marian from a faded photograph was slim ...she must have been deranged to concoct such an outlandish idea.

Of course, Marian wasn't her mother – that was the point. Her deathbed disclosure was so cruel. Why had she not told her years ago? Why wait until the last moment when it was impossible to give details or justify the abandonment by her real family? Anger burned in the pit of her stomach, yet she couldn't sustain this much bitterness against someone she had loved.

Suddenly alone, in the only home she'd ever known, Terry had fantasised before the funeral. A stranger would be among the mourners, claiming her, weeping for the lost years! Gradually she succumbed to a growing anger with the faceless person who had given her away. Finally, in church, she wept, lamenting the loss of Marian who had cherished her. Being adopted was unimportant – she'd never lacked love.

As time passed, her initial frustration returned. Surrounded by Marian's possessions, although legally in possession, Terry felt alien. If only Marian hadn't created doubt, the authenticity of her birth certificate would never have been questioned …baby Theresa, mother Marian, and father James Jones.

Instead of dismissing the confession, Terry brooded. Why had Marian not taken her secret to the grave? Knowing her end was near, had she been overcome with guilt? Terry agonised over the mystery and interrogated Marian's sister, as they perused family albums.

Picking up the only photo in the album of Marian as a young woman, she realised that the man standing next to her must be James. She examined it in silence, while Phyllis fidgeted.

Phyllis smoothed her grey hair nervously. "It's so long ago, dear," she protested. "We never, ever, referred to it, but I suppose there's no harm discussing it now." She was clearly disconcerted and fussed with the tea trolley before resuming. "Jim desperately wanted a family and deserted Marian after she'd had several miscarriages. They weren't living here when they divorced, they were up north." She began to fidget again and Terry prompted impatiently, "He obviously didn't love her!"

"You could be right, in the end," her aunt agreed. "I never forgave him. Anyway, later, when Marian brought you home, we assumed he was your father and that he'd left before knowing she was pregnant. Served him right, we thought." Seeing Terry's bewilderment, Phyllis added hastily, "Oh, he really wasn't that bad and Marian didn't seem to hold a grudge. She devoted herself to you. Years later, when she told me you were not her natural child, I was shocked but agreed not to tell anyone."

"But my birth certificate gives no hint of adoption..." Terry hesitated, appalled. Had she been a substitute for their own miscarried child – stolen from another couple? "How terrible," she wailed, "perhaps I was kidnapped!" Even as the words were uttered, she couldn't believe that Marian would have inflicted such pain on another woman. Phyllis knew nothing more and hope of discovering her origin receded, but Terry persevered. "Where was she living when she was supposed to have given birth?"

"Spain."

"Spain!" Terry was stunned. "I can't recall her ever leaving England, even on a day trip. Now you're saying she actually lived abroad. Where, for God's sake?"

"Somewhere on the Costa Blanca," Phyllis said, gazing at the atlas Terry immediately produced, "on that bit jutting out ...can't remember the name; something like gate, or gorgeous." Terry pointed and Phyllis delightedly agreed, "Yes, Gata de Gorgos, but does it really matter?"

Terry pretended it didn't matter, but had immediately started planning this birthday treat for herself – a Spanish holiday. She'd been gripped by the notion that someone here might remember Marian and Jim and reveal her past.

Yesterday, the 'Lemon Express' had brought her sedately northwards from Alicante, trundling along the burnished coast of the Mediterranean.

The fierce sunshine, reflecting back from clusters of white painted houses, was almost blinding without dark glasses and, as the train passed orchards and acres of terraced vines or clung tenaciously to winding hills, Terry, was entranced.

Alighting at Gata's tiny station she swung her backpack over her shoulders and walked the short distance to the main thoroughfare.

Enquiries, over coffee in a roadside bar, had led her to rent this room – no problem out of season. The house was immaculate and cool. Thick walls and small windows afforded protection from seasonal extremes and the bed was as comfortable as any she'd ever slept in. Night traffic rumbling to and from the Valencia/Alicante autopista hadn't bothered Terry but her need for sleep battled with the excitement of knowing that this was where her real family had lived ...or still lived.

Sunlight began dappling through the lace curtains before she dozed fitfully but when shouting in the street below indicated that her birthday had officially begun, she rose with relief.

By the time she'd freshened up and had breakfast, shops, mostly selling wickerwork or ceramics, were opening everywhere – dozens of them! How could all make a living when their wares, spilling onto the pavements, were so similar? Terry window-shopped each way, dodging heavy traffic to embrace both sides. Bars everywhere staked claim to their frontage with colourful umbrellas to protect small tables that spilled out from their dark, cool interiors. Cars mounted kerbs, parking wherever there was space.

Terry spent the morning exploring, away from the main road. Sombrely clad, local women, gossiped in groups outside the open doors of their homes, sitting on uncomfortably upright chairs. Most of them were busily knitting or lace-making but all stared inquisitively as she circumvented them, longing to interrupt.

Occasionally, taking advantage of a shy smile,

she thrust the photograph of a young Marian at them and in phrase book Spanish, tried to explain her quest. Followed by their regrets she wandered deeper into the narrow alleys. Shielded by terraced houses, few streets, even at noon, were penetrated by sunlight. Wrought iron streetlamps swung on brackets. Their linking wires banded together to traverse the whitewashed walls, skirting balconies, windows and glass-fronted shrines, some adorned by fresh flowers.

Decorative iron grills protected every window and flowers burst through the bars in profusion from pots on tiled sills. Some house doors were open and occasionally Terry glimpsed inner courtyards full of plants. Who would have suspected that secluded gardens sheltered behind the high facades? By the time she found a few shops they were closing for the afternoon siesta.

In the maze of cobbled walkways, unchanged for generations, Terry's imagination re-created a past, despite knowing she was unlikely to discover hers – she could hardly knock on every door! Her deep desire to belong welled up, blinding her with tears, making her dizzy.

"Buenos dia señorita ...Pero ...¿ qué pasa?" A woman, her old face creased in concern, emerged magically from a nearby doorway. Her shouts produced a chair, which she offered, *"¡Sientate!"*

"Muchas gracias." Terry sat gratefully,

accepting a glass of water. *"Y lo siento,"* she apologised. The realisation that she was English created a flurry and young Juan was pulled forward to meet her.

He said, "You are well now?" The lilt in his voice transformed the statement into a question and Terry, thankful that her poor Spanish wouldn't be needed, blamed her faintness on the heat.

"Hoy hace mucho calor," his grandmother agreed, prompting him to offer help.

It was too good a chance to miss. Terry produced her photograph to explain her apparent madness, wandering in the burning sun. It was examined until all heads shook in unison and Juan returned it. What else had she expected!

"I take you to shop of Señora Lopez. She know Gata whole life – you show, when open."

Terry knew she'd have hours to wait but, thanking them profusely, she insisted on leaving and accompanied Juan to a corner shop she had seen earlier …but it was a hardware store! She could have sworn it was a ceramica. She must have been hallucinating long before her collapse.

After he'd gone, she leaned against the wide sill of the stone porch still feeling slightly dizzy. Time passed, until hunger prodded her into wakefulness. She needed to eat but suddenly realised that the grill was open and the door ajar.

Voices issued from inside and, peeping into

the dim interior, she saw someone being served.

Terry smiled at the girl behind the counter as she entered and waited. She'd expected to be surrounded by tools and cooking equipment, but the shelves were crowded with decorative pottery and above – marked for sale – pictures hung on the walls. While admiring the display she followed the conversation fairly well and was disappointed to hear that the owner, Señora Lopez? was away. The young woman patted her swollen stomach …yes – she would return very soon because today her grandchild would be born!

There seemed no point in waiting, but she saw a painting she was tempted to buy …the customer picked it up before she could reach it! The artist, the girl boasted, was her husband Hymee Honess.

Terry was inexplicably overcome by a wave of nausea and escaped into the fresh air. Outside, resting on the ledge, she decided to treat herself to a painting – a lasting memento. If the customer bought that one, there must be others by Honess.

Glancing back, she saw the grill closed and padlocked. She had seen nobody leave and was amazed how quickly and quietly she'd been locked out.

No matter, there was always tomorrow. *Mañana*! She felt strangely tranquil. Her search for her past seemed less urgent; Spain was already working its magic. She would return at the end of her holiday when she'd know how much money she could afford.

On the edge of town, she found a tapas bar. The tasty snacks were of such variety that her appetite was satisfied. The piercing warbles of caged birds became inaudible as crowds and vehicles returned to the streets after sunset. Voices at top volume competed with a cacophony of music but Terry was too exhausted to join the revellers. *Mañana*, she promised wryly as she returned to her room.

During the following days, walking, swimming or beach combing, Terry felt an exhilarating sense of well-being and although she had abandoned her search, she didn't regret coming.

On her last day, she estimated how much she could spend and returned to the gallery.

When she entered, she felt disorientated … had she come to the wrong place? It was well lit and colourful. Vases, dishes and ornaments were everywhere. Wall shelves had replaced hanging space. There were no pictures. She turned towards the counter where the mother-to-be had stood. She was still there, staring back, wide eyed. No! A mirror was throwing back her own image. Her dark shining hair, upswept for coolness, helped the illusion but she couldn't doubt that her smooth olive skin, now tanned, and melting dark eyes were inherited features …features identical to the girl who had been serving. They were of the same family: Terry had to meet her, to belong, to have a past as well as a future.

The elderly receptionist seemed baffled when asked about the assistant who was pregnant. Terry, blaming her own inadequate translation, asked when Señora Lopez would return.

"But I am she," came the response in halting English, "I not away. How can I do for you?"

Dazed, Terry dumbly offered the photographs for examination. When the woman said she knew him many years ago – it was Hymee Honess, Terry blanched. How could she have been so stupid! To her he was James Jones and the Spanish pronunciation had meant nothing to her. The woman invited her to sit. "The lady is Madame Honess, sister of Hymee – she take baby of Maria after they die." She looked at the calendar and gasped, "On today, two weeks after baby comes, their house is burning! And I in Valencia, cannot help"

Terry's mind reeled.

On her birthday, she had seen her mother's ghost, merely hours before her own birth! Two weeks later Marian claimed her, Jim's ex-wife, not his sister! Everyone had obviously been misled by the name. Terry eventually explained who she was and Señora Lopez cried with delight, hugging her. She excused herself shakily and wobbled up the narrow stairs to return, minutes later, carrying an oil painting, the one Terry had seen before.

"Here, my gift for you," the señora smiled, pointing to the signature. "See! Hymee Honess, your father!" Her vision of Maria might have been a dream brought on by heatstroke and a similar painting in Marian's bedroom must also be by her father although she'd never noticed! Had that picture triggered her vision of this one? Others might question her strange experience, but Terry was at peace. At last, she felt complete.

Bye & Bye

Distantly, in his dream, Edward heard a child screaming for help. He struggled to hold on to his precious sleep until, as he slowly awoke, he realised that the cries were not in his head – they were real. When he had come to sit in the garden, the effort had made him regret agreeing to rest outside for a change. Supported by his daughter, Betty, his old bones seemed to creak as he sank onto the cushioned, wicker chair. She took good care of him and had sent eight-year old Pamela out for a few hours, to give him some peace.

Now, the petrifying thought that his granddaughter might be in trouble brought him fully awake and he pushed himself to sit, then stand, as he shouted for Betty. When she didn't appear, he turned towards the river ...the wails were more desperate and, without thought to his own infirmity, Edward hurried to the field gate.

The river twisted away just beyond the garden and, under the steep bank where the surging water had carved a deep trench, he saw a little girl clinging to some exposed tree roots. It was not Pamela, but, as he registered the thought with relief, she slipped a few feet farther away. He almost ran to reach her, fear making him forgetful of his own condition …he had to save her; there was no one else in sight.

He clung to a low bough and lowered himself over the edge. The child sobbed her relief, "Oh, Mr. Lodge, I was so afraid. I thought nobody would come and I'd die." Edward recognised her as one of Pam's young friends. He could see that she was too terrified to reach for the dipping branch herself and gritted his teeth …he'd have to wade in. With difficulty, he removed his heavy cardigan and flung it up onto the grass – it was cumbersome and would be more useful dry than wet.

The current was strong as it swept round the bend, but he inched as far as he dared along the bough and succeeded in clamping his hand round the girl's slender wrist.

"Come on, Jenny. We'll soon have you back on dry land," he assured her as he hauled them both out of danger. She was exhausted and hardly any help at all as he pushed her up to safety, over the jutting embankment. He waded to where it was lower, then scrambled up to join the shaking child. He was muddy up to his knees but not unduly uncomfortable. Enfolding her in the warm jacket Edward sat and comforted her until she stopped sobbing. "We must get you home, young lady," he said, helping her to her feet. "Where do you live?"

It crossed his mind that she seemed reasonably normal now; perhaps he could safely leave her, when they reached the road. It was many years since he had been out alone; Betty would be frantic when she couldn't find him. His walking days were a distant memory, but he didn't feel too stressed, in spite of his exertions. In fact, he suddenly felt adventurous and began moving towards the village, holding Jenny's hand. Relief had loosened her tongue and she babbled without expecting a reply. She was looking for pebbles to paint and had overreached for a particularly large one. The current had carried her, "For miles," she said. "I can swim a bit, but the water was so fast I thought I was going to drown. Then I bumped against that bank and managed to hold on." She smiled up at him and squeezed his hand shyly. "You saved my life."

They skirted the village and entered streets that he had known well when he was young. He was thrilled to see his old school still in use but now smartened and enlarged – no longer just for infants. Before they reached Jenny's home, they passed an old cottage where his best friend had lived. For a moment he could have sworn he saw Joe's grandmother smiling at him from the window; she would have to be about a hundred and forty by now, he chuckled.

Jenny's mother was aghast when she heard

how close she had been to losing her only child and invited Edward to stay at least for a few moments to rest, but he declined. Apart from the fact that he wanted to get home, he was enjoying revisiting his old haunts. "But I would be grateful if you'd ring my daughter," he suggested, "she may have missed me by now. Tell her I'm fine, and on my way back."

The street was more populated when he emerged. Several older people waved and some even addressed him by name...

"Good to see you again Eddie," said a familiar voice and he turned to see a wartime comrade, instantly recognisable. The man had hardly changed and, as they spoke animatedly, Edward stared at his dark, curly hair and remembered the beach at Dunkirk.

He began to feel confused...

Betty answered the telephone and listened as Jenny's mother expressed her gratitude for the timely rescue and said Mr Lodge was on his way home. "I don't understand," she shook her head and fought back her tears. "You must be mistaken. My father could hardly stand alone, never mind walk. And, anyway, I'm afraid he died last week. He just fell asleep in the garden... Yes, a very peaceful death. Please don't apologise, you couldn't have known." Betty replaced the receiver quietly.

Impossible though it seemed, she felt calmer and less miserable than she had since finding him. His favourite hymn, sung at his funeral, ran through her head and she could almost hear him singing it now…

"In the swe-ee-eet… Bye and By-y-ye… We shall meet on that Beautiful Shore…"

… and was suddenly sure that, one day, they really would meet again.

Checking the Facts

I really would love to be a writer, but writers have to know things, like what people do when they sit at a piano ‑ practise or practice, c or s ‑ and that the other is, or is definitely not, what a doctor has.

Actually, I tried looking it up once. Tearing myself away from my word processor and the gripping plot I was devising, I searched the bookshelf for anything musical or medical ‑ no luck! While I looked through a heap of magazines, continually side-tracked by letters written by desperate housewives to the problem pages, the electricity failed. Naturally, I read on, happily unaware that because I hadn't *"SAVED"*, my words were lost and all my devoted research a waste of time!

Later, when the power returned, I gave up fuming and sat at the keyboard again, trying to reconstruct it. Everything was working except my brain! I seriously thought I must have dreamed about having written the perfect outline for the great masterpiece of the century ‑ the one that would be awarded a prize for "Best Selling First

Novel By A New Writer" or something, because I had totally lost the plot ...and it had been a brilliant opening line! Then I saw that the time on my watch didn't agree with the electric clock – the one I had been keeping an eye on so that I wouldn't be late with the lunch again!

The rattle of keys and the front door slamming sent me into a panic. Switching off the computer and restoring his desk to its usual state – littered – I almost broke my neck to reach the kitchen and look busy before he emerged from the hall cloakroom.

When I am a Best-Selling Author, I'll have a cook/housekeeper!

I never did remember all the brilliant twists and turns of the story I'd worked out that morning, but the outline I decided to be happy with, proved disastrous. It was the 1980s, for goodness sake, so why I wove my story around life circa 1920 I shall never understand – history was never my strong point at school, although it was marginally better than my geography, which ranked low, alongside science and maths. I suppose I had imagined that having living links to the era through a heap of elderly relatives, it would be easy to sound convincing.

In an attempt to revive my enthusiasm for the story, a brilliant idea popped into my head. I could take my tiny, unobtrusive cassette recorder on visits to old aunts and uncles who would welcome me as a diversion from their usual boring chores and willingly sit for hours, talking over old times.

Deciding to start with my parents, because they lived closest, I rang to tell them my plans and said I'd be round in twenty minutes. I could hear Mum explaining it to Dad, sounding suitably excited and his reply, which wasn't flattering so I won't repeat it.

To be fair, I know that in the past I have started a good many schemes and embarked on projects that were never completed, but this time is different. I am determined to write a book. I heard him reminding her that she wanted him to dig up some potatoes but she, always eager to encourage me, told him, "Never mind, we'll have a tin of spaghetti for lunch," and to me, she said they were both thrilled to help and she'd put the kettle on straight away.

Later, while we drank coffee, Dad relaxed and they both giggled as they recalled their courting days. They revealed quite a lot about the years of their youth, in the early decades of the century and I was so enthralled I forgot about the recorder, until Mum said, "I'll just clear away the tray, then we'll get down to work."

When she came back, I showed off the dinky little gadget, switched it on and set it facing them where they sat together on the settee. They did try to get back into the mood, but it was hopeless. After ten minutes of embarrassed elbowing and throat clearing, Dad said he'd better get the spuds after all ...it looked like rain!

The following day I took my recorder to visit Aunt Amy and Uncle Jim. They are in their eighties, so I didn't bother to ring first. I did not want them worrying about my visit, or fussily making a special event of it; better to surprise them, I decided.

Instead of looking delighted, when she saw me on the doorstep she said, looking distinctly upset, "I thought it was Freda at last! We are all waiting to play – the morning will be gone at this rate! How is your bridge, child?"

She clucked with disappointment, when told it was non-existent, and was not at all enthusiastic when I explained the purpose of my visit. She said I could ask Uncle Jim for his help, he had more spare time than she did, but I'd have to come another day – he was out at a stamp-club auction.

To avoid a wasted morning (in spite of my aunt's panic it was still only 10.30!), I caught a bus out of town to the old peoples' home where the Godfather of our clan was winding up his days. Grandfather used to tell us stories by the hour, when we were kids. He was never too tired at the end of his working day to take one of us on his lap and talk about the funny, naughty things he'd done at school. Pranks that he and his friends had played on their teachers were high on our list of favourites and we believed every word as fervently as we did the Gospel. Actually, I had intended saving Grandfather for the last, sure of his enthusiasm and full co-operation, but I was in dire need of a mental boost before my own interest in the subject waned.

He was really pleased to see me. An orderly wheeled him out into the garden, to enjoy the unusually sunny day, and we settled down for a nice private chat.

As he was able to walk, he was upset about being in the chair and used up fifteen minutes telling me how fit he actually was and how they insisted on cosseting him, just because he was ninety-eight! They just wanted to show him off when he reached a hundred, he said. "They think they are all going to be interviewed with me on television... only another eighteen months to go you know, and I'm as good as ever I was – well nearly!"

Not sure how to interpret his nudge-nudge wink-wink, I hastily produced my recorder and explained why I wanted to talk to him. The miniature wonder fascinated him so much I had to show him how it worked. He spent the next ten minutes playing with it and succeeded in wiping the admittedly few comments I had actually managed to record!

The matron, warning me not to tire him, had graciously given us an hour together. Half the time had already gone and I was exhausted. He was as bright as a button and, having pressed record, he held the thing an inch from his nose and proceeded to shout into it.

Forcibly pulling his hand farther away from his mouth (and turning the volume down) did not noticeably interrupt his flow as he embarked on his life history. I was suddenly optimistic that usable material would result from what, so far, had been a fiasco.

My hopes were dashed when he reached ten-years-old and got stuck in the old groove of school scrapes. "Very funny," I interrupted yet again, "but what was your home like? What did your parents do for evening entertainment or at weekends? What was their life like?"

He looked at me in astonishment and sniffed – "Life? Oh, their life? Ordinary, same as everybody else's. Now school – that was exciting! Didn't learn a lot, me and my mates, but we had a great time! Did I ever tell you about the time we locked the headmaster in a cupboard?"

Last week I had a brilliant idea for a new plot and, if ever the bus comes, I'm on my way to the library to check up on a few things. That's what I mean – real writers don't have to waste time going out for information, they have all they need in their heads. It is such a waste of time standing here when I could be enjoying myself at the word processor – moving paragraphs around, inserting, deleting and finally counting how many words I've written. There is nothing more gratifying than seeing the word total growing by thousand after thousand.

Still no bus: I'm going home! I know that quality is more important than quantity – I'm not stupid, but surely whoever edits it will correct spelling mistakes and make sure the facts are right... Isn't that what editors are for?

Crime de la Crème

Would it be a crime, Gerry wondered, to finish off the leftover cream with the leftover strawberries …after all, it was barely a single portion. He would have eaten it when they entertained on Sunday, if Brenda hadn't told everyone that he'd put himself on a diet and was being very strong-minded about it.

Now miles away, spending a week with her parents, Brenda wouldn't expect the cream to keep and wasn't around to see his lapse, so he poured it over the rich, red fruit, to enjoy later.

She was so organised. Extra steak and vegetables had been cooked when preparing for their guests, "But you won't want the same meal two nights in a row," she had stated as he departed for the office the following morning. "I've prepared chicken casserole and rice pudding – enough for tonight and Wednesday. The timer is set, it will be ready at six-thirty, so don't be late. Eat the steak and leftovers tomorrow." Without pausing for his agreement, she reminded him that he'd been invited to dine with friends on

Thursday and there was a frozen pizza he could microwave on Friday. "If I'm not back in time to cook on Saturday, we'll eat out," she declared.

Gerry had enjoyed the casserole and pudding last night, after an exhausting day – Mondays were always hectic. He reflected that, in spite of her bossiness, he was lucky to have Brenda who had gone out of her way to leave him his favourite meal on her first night away. The mouth-watering aroma greeted him as he'd walked in through the front door. Tonight, as he re-heated the steak (just a quick flip over in a hot pan, she had advised) he felt twinges of guilt. Not about the cream: adultery was a much worse sin. Lucille wouldn't have stood a chance, if Brenda had been as passionate after their marriage as she'd been before. So, although it was really her fault, he had no intention of leaving her. She was ideal in every other way.

Sunday's dinner had been nerve-wracking. He was amused when Brenda first decided to find an ideal mate for Tom, his 'best man' two years ago.

When Tom's own plans to marry disintegrated, Brenda started including him whenever they entertained, but he'd shown no interest in Brenda's beauty parade until she'd invited Lucille.

Gerry tried to convince her, to no avail, that bringing his secretary into their home life was a mistake; he had hardly spoken to Lucille on that first visit; his equilibrium shattered by the strain of keeping aloof. One unguarded glance or over-familiar word would have alerted Brenda to the true nature of their relationship. Lucille had been so anxious to conceal it, she hardly took her eyes off Tom, hanging on his every word! The poor sap was convinced that she had fallen for him and asked Gerry to invite them together as often as possible. Commenting on Gerry's obvious reluctance to encourage him, he jokingly wondered if Gerry had a 'thing' going with her himself – fortunately out of Brenda's hearing!

He recalled the day Tom saw them lunching together at a pricey hotel, well removed from the quick-snack route. Tom managed a garden centre and was apparently contracted to maintain the plants and floral decorations in the public rooms. If only he'd known, he would have avoided the place – there were plenty others. He'd quickly explained, "My secretary and I have been entertaining clients," but Tom's sharp eyes strayed around the small table, obviously set only for two. "...In the bar," Gerry, equally alert, added, "so we decided to eat here to save time."

Tom obviously remembered the occasion, so Gerry had to appear enthusiastic about helping him in his pursuit of Lucille and, as the weeks passed, he grew accustomed to their presence as a pair. They made up tables of six or eight, or a four for bridge, and it was dangerously exciting in a way, being so near to her, under Brenda's unsuspecting eye. It amused Lucille to play up to Tom. Privately, during extended lunch hours or late nights 'working' together, she left him in no doubt that, with Tom, she was only playing games, but the atmosphere on Sunday had been different somehow. Brenda kept questioning Lucille. How did she feel about marriage? Surely, if she wanted children, she should be finding a husband! Even Tom was on edge and followed Brenda to the kitchen, ostensibly removing dishes from the table but, Gerry was sure, warning Brenda to drop the subject.

They both returned looking subdued and the other guests departed earlier than usual. Perhaps it signalled an end to Brenda's matchmaking – he hoped!

He fried a couple of eggs to eat with the steak and avoided having butter with his potatoes to make up for the calories in the cream. He wasn't all that unhappy with his figure. Brenda said it was perfect. Lucille was more critical and teased him about his rounding belly.

Remembering her laughter, as he lifted his dessert from the fridge, he regretted having already covered the fruit and even considered washing the cream off, but some of the berries had fallen apart and would be rendered inedible. Oh dear, he would have to risk getting fat after all, he sighed, smirking, as he carried them to the table and picked up his spoon.

Brenda's parents were happy for her to visit old school friends who would be upset, she reminded them, if she didn't call to admire their babies, homes, or just enjoy a good gossip. All those who were still single asked what had happened to that dishy 'Best Man' "...Forget him," she advised, "Gerry's secretary has her eye on him – they are practically an item!"

Even as she spoke, she pictured Lucille, not with Tom, but with Gerry. Would he really eat at home, or take her out for intimate dinners somewhere? She didn't really care what Gerry did, with or without his precious secretary, as she pictured Tom waiting for her at the motel.

In spite of their instant mutual attraction when their eyes had met over her groom's shoulder in front of the altar, only during these last few days had they spent more than a stolen half-hour together.

Guilt at her change of heart kept her faithful to her marriage vows until she'd realised that Gerry was having an affair with the luscious Lucille. She knew she shouldn't blame him as he must have sensed the difference in her, but she was outraged and eventually gave in to Tom's entreaties to meet him, far away from home, of course.

Tom told her about the scrap of conversation he'd overheard when he found them lunching together; they wished her dead.

She was devastated.

Divorce was easy these days; so why should they be so cruel? True, Gerry had been impoverished when they first met, but his business was thriving now, even if he wasn't yet out of debt. She, on the other hand, still had a sizeable portion of an inheritance left – even after buying the house he had chosen. Even though it was all too clear why her demise was preferable to any other solution, she refused to believe that Gerry would harm her in any way.

Tom worried that he might and tried to convince her how easy it would be to turn the tables. When he'd helped her to clear the table on Sunday, he produced a tiny bottle full of milky liquid, reminding her that he had a range of lethal garden chemicals at his disposal. Naturally, she didn't take him seriously; hoping someone would die was a long way from actually committing murder!

Shaken by even the hint that Tom would act so rashly, she agreed to spend some time with him while visiting her parents. He was so sensitive and had realised how upset she had been all evening. She'd as good as told Lucille to find her own man and marry him! In that vulnerable state she was easily persuaded that her duty visit home was a perfect opportunity for them to relax together.

Tom, used to looking after himself, was quite domesticated. He'd helped her to sort what could be saved from what couldn't and commented, as he scraped the last of the cream into a plastic container, that in spite of Gerry's diet he would probably rather enjoy it than waste it.

He watched as she stacked it away with the rest of the food she'd prepared for Gerry and couldn't resist commenting on how lucky the idiot was; he didn't deserve her.

As Brenda walked from her car to the room where Tom was waiting, she prayed that she wouldn't be recognised by anyone. It was no good telling herself that she shouldn't feel guilty. She was committing adultery and was ashamed. The fact that Gerry had committed the same crime first was no excuse and she was adamant that after this week she would not see Tom alone again.

Later, when she told him he didn't argue. Surely, he hadn't tired of her so soon she thought! Sensing her astonishment, Tom hastily assured her that he appreciated how much against her nature it had been for her to give in to his selfishness. He held her tightly and whispered, "These precious days will be our secret. There'll never be anyone else. I'll be here whenever you need me." Brenda was comforted. If only her religious convictions allowed her to divorce Gerry, she wouldn't have needed to swap the contents of Tom's little bottle, for milk. She knew that Tom, unfortunately, had been joking but, unlike him, she had no qualms about using it when the time came.

As Tom watched Brenda leave, he wondered how long it would be before news reached her of Gerry's tragic death. He might not be found for days but no suspicion would fall on Brenda. He'd been worried to see her on the point of emptying it down the sink but had convinced her he could never commit such a dreadful crime. As soon as she'd left the kitchen, he had emptied it himself – all over the cream!

She was far too sweet and gentle to believe him capable of murder. What a wonderful life they were going to enjoy together ... Gerry had never appreciated how lucky he was!

Echoes

The grey pre-dawn shadows lifted, and light seeped relentlessly through his heavy eyelids. He endured the hardness of the rifle in the protective folds of his thaub, bruising his ribs; it must be clean and ready – free of the clinging dust, which he could feel in every pore. Physical discomfort could be ignored, but memory and habit carried to his inner ear the call of the Imam. The swelling and fading chant echoing from the minaret in his now distant village was too far to be audible. Awareness of the coming day forced him to consciousness and the realisation that where he lay there was no mosque ...no uplifting voice to inspire him when his need was so great.

He unwrapped the gun and rested it, carefully, in the dry branches of a long-dead bush that had seemed to offer protection when, wearily, he'd huddled close to it, the night before. After rubbing his feet and hands with the powdery sand to cleanse them, he lifted his ghutrah from his head, spread it on the ground and knelt on it – facing Mecca, to seek and find peace in his God.

He stayed kneeling, even after his prayer ended – mesmerised by the beauty of the desert.

Shadowed tufts of arfaj, that had escaped grazing camels, were crowned with speckled halos of gold as the light strengthened.

His thoughts drifted to his childhood, when he first saw this wilderness transformed after a single shower of rain. With little encouragement, delicate buds grew and burst into glorious life, blazing briefly before shrivelling in the fierce sun – rarely seen by human eyes. Like men, they occupied a small space for a blink of eternity and then passed unnoticed; fierce winds smoothing the places where all live and die. In the way of the Bedu, he understood the desert and was never lost in its shifting dunes. He loved this emptiness, where his ancestors had existed for generations ...where his own family was wiped out so cruelly.

The savage horsemen who stormed in that day were Arabs, like themselves. He had peeped from the bait ash sha'ar, lifting the heavy woven cloth, made from the wool of their own goats by his mother and sisters who had also erected the tent. They'd hauled and secured the yards of brown-striped fabric to stout poles, to protect them all from the elements. The women were always working and even at four-years-old he was grateful to Allah for making him a man.

He had been excited when the strangers

arrived – too innocent to perceive their haughty demeanour – and watched with pride, as his father and older brothers greeted them ..."As salaam alaikum," God's peace be upon you. Then, without warning, the horsemen drew their long swords. At first, he was more astonished than afraid, but when they'd lunged about with flashing blades, he scrambled from hiding into the burning midday heat, desperate to find reassurance with his mother ...Safety lay in her arms.

Terrified by the anguished shrieking all around, he ran back, but never reached his goal ...the entire tent crashed to the ground.

On waking, he felt smothered; the pole that had struck him pinned him down. Crazed with fear he struggled from mountains of cloth to find air then, free at last and still unable to see, he screamed in terror, but the darkness was not in his eyes it belonged to the night. In anguish, he wailed all his loved ones' names into the stillness but heard no answer. Sobbing, he stumbled over familiar things, out of place, and in that strangeness fell suddenly into arms he knew. His cries became moans of joy – but why did his mother not speak?

Why was she so cold?

Seized by panic he ran into the black void, away from his grotesquely transformed world, into the real unknown. The tiny child collapsed at last until the coldness of dawn stung him to wakefulness and he recognised the outline of an old fort. His father had often taken him there to seek advice from the elder who existed in the ruins. Wise Ali Ibrahim was loved by all his people; when he told the old man about the horsemen, surely everything would be put right.

In a way they were. After listening to the boy Ali returned with him to the camp where he'd known many friends and they wept in each other's arms. Then, as Khalid's tears dried, Ali told him who the evil men were and why their tribe hated his own.

Forcing the stunned child to look at his mutilated family until their dreadful wounds were etched permanently into his brain, Ali explained that his enemies did this to all who dared to disagree with them. The scene was unreal to Khalid; reality was the hatred, which would burn inside him forever.

Until the old man took him there to start his new life, he had been wary of the village and its people who lived so differently from his own. They need not wander with their goats and camels ...they had a good well, a small oasis with green bushes and dusty stone houses, whose strong walls protected them from the fierce winds that raged from the north. He soon became as much a part of his new family as the other sons and, as the years passed, his visits to Ali Ibrahim – a whole day's camel ride away – were irregular. If the sessions had not always ended with a prayer for his family and vengeance, he might have forgotten that he was born to another tribe. Although he loved Ali, on whom he relied for spiritual guidance, such words seemed empty to him ...what could he, a mere boy, do against grown men, in their dozens and armed to the teeth!

As he developed into a slim, handsome youth, Khalid's ardour was fired by Ali's entreaties to Allah, but his feelings of impotence increased so, suppressing his guilt, his treks to the fort became fewer.

Hearing one day that the old man was near death, remorse made him hurry to Ali's side ...how could he have neglected his beloved teacher?

What could he do for him now, unworthy being that he was? They both knew it would be their final encounter. The ancient face was haggard with pain and in whispered gasps the dying sage reminded him of the duty he owed to his forebears.

They lamented, recalling the wrecked site bereft of life until, in blind rage, Khalid cried out for a just revenge. The loathed names, whispered again from those dry thin lips, would abide with him until all who bore them paid with their own blood.

"Why?" Khalid had to know. "Why, did the horsemen slaughter so wantonly? Are we not Arabs too?"

"There are Arabs and Arabs," said Ali, "not all are true believers."

"How can we be sure ours is the true path?" he'd asked.

"Did they not butcher your father because his ideas were different? Is that acceptable? Their actions prove them wrong ...so it follows, we are right. Allah is with the righteous and gives us strength."

"It is said," answered Khalid – more than a little frightened by his own daring, "that vengeance belongs to Allah."

"Did not Allah also bid you leave your home to fight for true justice? Are you not willing to be his instrument?"

His promise never to forget was given with passion but he had been barely sixteen; living, gradually obscured his distant past.

Many moons after Ali's death, soldiers came to the village.

The stubby guns they carried seemed more menacing than Khalid's old hunting rifle, but the men were friendly and joked with him. At first their words perplexed him, but he soon grasped that they were speaking his own tongue in a strange way.

They were welcomed everywhere. They played games with children, sat smoking companionably with old men and bought from the souq. Khalid hovered on the fringe of their affairs wishing they would stay forever but, after a few days, they prepared to move on. Like soldiers everywhere the men were easy and secure with each other and he gazed after them enviously as they sauntered away to their more important world.

He followed, to their amusement, trailing ever farther behind, reluctant to be free of the spell they cast yet knowing he must return.

When something flashed in the waning sunlight, as it fell in their wake, he searched the trampled sand eagerly; returning it would be an excuse to join them again. There! He pounced, triumphant, but was stunned – dizzy with horror – when he beheld the loop of shiny beads in his palm. His father, lost in thought, had constantly played with this same chain, swinging it back and forth over his hand. Khalid stared aghast at the glowing amber stone he'd found as a small child and presented with pride one feast day after Ramadan.

The solders' strident voices carried back to him over the still air – raucous, calling each other by name – reviled names, suddenly remembered with sickness and revulsion.

He almost swooned, knowing that these men belonged to the tribe whose crimes he'd sworn to avenge. He now perceived how they'd swaggered, weapons held ready, obviously feeling superior.

How they must have sniggered at the simple villagers – mocking smiles covering the scorn they must have felt for the old way of life. Then icy fear gripped him ...would they return? Would they come swooping on horseback to kill and kill again, wiping out all he loved as they had done before?

He had to stop them.

They were on foot, so their camp must be near; following would be easy with no wind to disturb their tracks. Even so, he hurried as he went back to fetch his rifle.

He wished he'd used his small supply of bullets more sparingly but vowed that the last few would not be wasted. After filling his water pouch, he drew a cloak over his shoulders; the desert could be cruelly cold at night and the fur-lined bisht was essential as he had no idea how long he would be away. The sun, a blood-red disc, was already sliding rapidly into the dark purple horizon as he left home. There was no hope of catching the patrol before nightfall, but it didn't matter; he guessed that the old fort with its sweet water well was their refuge ...it would also be their grave. More than ever before, he needed to commune with Allah so left the trail to offer his evening prayer.

After ritual cleansing, he stood for a moment, head bowed in the flat, failing light before falling to his knees. Long practice enabled him to clear his mind of earthly problems until his prayer ended, leaving him calmly convinced that he was fulfilling his destiny. Images of death returned to feed his righteous anger.

As he trudged through the darkness, he saw himself again as a tiny child holding his father's hand, comforted by its gentle strength. He had been a kindly man, who never spoke of war or reprisal and shielded his children from such knowledge, but Ali Ibrahim was more shrewd and worldly; he knew that learning must be passed on.

Khalid was grateful to have had such a teacher to show him right from wrong – making his enemies known to him so that his hatred was not allowed to die. Another sun came and waned before he yielded to sleep, within reach of the fort.

Waking, in the grip of a nameless dread, he rose stiffly; recollection returned. Cold air had even penetrated the cloak, which had served as a blanket; the heavy, morning mist covered it with a sparkling sheet of dew. He shook the wetness off it and spread it over the bush to dry, careful not to dislodge his gun. The sun was already warming the empty sky; it was for this coming day that he alone, of his whole family, had been preserved. He was the chosen instrument upon which Allah could play to wreak his will. The Divine plan was so clear to him now. His miraculous survival ...having a trusted friend to teach and guide him ...a new family to help him grow strong and, finally, being inspired to follow those vile creatures to hear the terrible names uttered. All the pieces had fallen into place; his people and his God would be proud of him.

Moving in the long shadows thrown by gold-edged hills over pale ochre sand he was soon within sight of the ancient ruins. He knew every broken wall, inside and out, having explored not only its present but, with old Ali's help, its past. He had learned about wise men long dead and battles fought hundreds of years before they were born.

"Why did those Christians come to fight us?" he once asked. The sage stroked his wispy beard and replied.

"Far away in their own land Christians still fight Christians – why should we be surprised that they once fought Arabs?"

He waited, hidden by the gnarled, twisted branches of an athl tree, to discover how many soldiers were within the old, stone walls. Just inside, he knew, was living space with a good roof where he had spent many happy hours. In his mind's eye he saw Ali Ibrahim sitting on the stone bench near the door. The bright rays of sunlight falling sharply over the folds of his robe were reflected upwards, lightening the shadows in his lined face. The memory moved him almost to tears.

The sun rose fully before he could be sure that all the men were present but his ears picked up the distant drone of a motor vehicle, sometimes clear, sometimes muffled but unmistakably coming nearer – spluttering and roaring as it struggled over hostile, shifting sand.

He was in a sweat of indecision. Should he wait or attack now? More soldiers were approaching: certainly too many to tackle alone. Or even worse, the truck might take away those still here to a place where he could not follow! He had to move. Whatever transpired he was still too far away to do anything.

From a better vantage point he saw them embracing each other as several prepared to leave. He was re-assured ...this too was fate. Allah in his mercy intended that only those most guilty should remain to die. The brief turmoil that ensued made it possible for him to slip quietly behind the outer wall through secret ways to the place where the guards would return. The room was smaller than he remembered – perhaps because it was now crammed with boxes, bedrolls and other comforts men always needed. A ray of sunlight slanted over the hollowed stone seat and he imagined he could still see white cloth draped over Ali's frail shoulders and his pale steady eyes, smiling encouragement.

Shouts outside banished his vision. The jovial taunts of those departing mingled with the grumbles of the few who must tarry but they would meet again soon they said ...*Inshalla.*"

They were calling on his God!

Now, hiding among the crates, so near his quarry, tremors of self-doubt shook him. The loaded gun felt awkward and almost slipped from his grasp. To bolster his resolve, he recalled the senseless carnage. His parents, brothers and sisters had not deserved death. These killers did! His eyes, growing used to the dimness, took in details previously missed. The embers of a dung fire still glowed, and the aroma of green cardamom coffee wafted from the long, curved beak of a pot resting in the hot ash. Had he come in peace he would have been offered a drink in one of the tiny cups, in the same spirit of hospitality that was part of his own tradition. Seeing rolled prayer mats against the wall he was torn again...! If they lived and prayed as he did, was he, after all, making a terrible mistake?

The truck pulled away and three men returned. Trembling with uncertainty, Khalid watched as two prepared for their afternoon rest, spreading rugs and goatskins on the hard-packed sand – their guns within reach. The third squatted in the cast shadow of the thick wall near the open door, his weapon across his knee. Khalid knew he would have time for only one shot before he was himself cut down, but it was not fear of death that made him hesitate. He stared along his rifle sight, not at a brutish enemy but at the fresh young face of a brother Arab ...the one whose buttermilk and laughter he had shared in the souq. How could he, after all, bring death to one of his own?

Sand swirled in from the burning desert heralding a Shamal and the guard threw a corner of his ghutrah across his face as the horsemen had. Fine dust spiralled upwards in the sunlight and Khalid suddenly saw old Ali Ibrahim: there, where he always sat. His gnarled hands clenched, he howled encouragement. His voice, echoing from the stones, merged with the wind...

"Have you forgotten the horsemen? These are their kin, our foes ...Shoot! Kill! Death to all who wrong us!"

Khalid must have fired. He saw the guard jerk forward to slump lifeless in the dust. As the others rolled towards him, guns blazing, he was deaf to their cries. He heard only sighs of pride from Ali, his friend who had not abandoned him, even in death. He was beckoning, smiling, waiting to guide him as rightly in the next life, as he had in this.

Flight of Fancy

Once upon a time, without ever having seen one, Lynne had believed in fairies. Now, in total *disbelief*, she was staring at one!

Ridiculous!

She almost lost her grip on her teacup. The clatter as it landed in the saucer, spilling a mercifully *small* drop of the remaining tea, convinced her that she was indeed awake.

She pushed her unruly dark fringe away from her eyes as she squeezed them shut for a moment. When she opened one, cautiously, her two-inch high visitor still sat on the lid of the butter dish eyeing her with equanimity. Delicate silver wings unfolded briefly, shimmering brightly in the kitchen gloom, to frame her slender body.

Lynne, never doubting her own sanity, decided that she was being deceived by a trick of the light and calmly assured herself that the anomaly would pass...

"Are you being deliberately impolite?"

The question interrupted her speculation, echoing thinly but clearly through her head and, although the creature was far too small for her to detect lip movement, she had no doubt that it was communicating. Her mouth opened partly in astonishment, but also in an instinctive attempt at denial. Yet, before she uttered a sound, the fairy, if that is what it was, replied.

"Good. I had to ask, because I'm not at all clever with words …and I'm not an 'it' either."

It was clear to Lynne that she had only to *think*, in order to participate in the exchange and she immediately tried to eliminate any stray thoughts that might be construed as offensive. She was already well on the way to accepting that, crazy or not, a fairy had dropped in for breakfast.

"Thank you, but I'm not hungry," echoed the reply to her unvoiced invitation and Lynne redoubled her efforts at self-control. This gave rise to a complaint, "…How can we be friends if you clam up?"

Good, Lynne congratulated herself; she was getting the hang of things.

"Yes, it is good. It's really warm and comfortable in here," said the fairy. Nodding towards the window, which was obscured by fast-running slashes of water, she declared, "It's raining so heavily outside, I nearly drowned." She fluttered her wings to dry them and inclined her head, picking up Lynne's amazement that she'd ventured out at all in such foul weather. "It wasn't raining when I started out," she said, "I've flown a long way and still have a few miles to go but I couldn't go on without a rest."

Lynne immediately wondered why she'd risked travelling so far. "Oh, to get far away from the city... I hate the smelly traffic, so I like to visit my country cousins. Your garden's full of flowers – it must be beautiful in the sunshine."

During the next half-hour, their conversation grew less stilted and they exchanged personal information about their families, hopes and aspirations. "What shall I call you?" Lynne asked, suddenly realising that they hadn't introduced each other.

"I haven't got a name. I've never needed one. Nobody calls me..."

She didn't seem particularly distressed, but Lynne was astonished and spoke aloud. "Well, fancy – no name!"

"Yes, call me Fancy," said the fairy, "I like that, Fancy Noname. Now I'll know when I'm called, thank you."

It was difficult to conceal her amusement so, before it could be picked up and upset her delightful guest, Lynne hastily asked about Fancy's family. Apparently, it was large, but they didn't live together. Sighing heavily, Fancy professed to envying Lynne who had a husband and two children, all under one roof. Yes, it must be hard work – cleaning, cooking, washing and ironing, but it might be worth it, just to be human.

She laughed at Lynne's fleeting thought … "No, I wouldn't do all my chores by magic!"

Lynne eyed her suspiciously. All the fairies she'd ever read about were able to cast spells and, by the way, did fairies still grant wishes? Apparently they did, under certain circumstances… if they were rescued from certain death, for instance, or cared-for during a long illness. Providing shelter from inclement weather was clearly a non-starter. "Just my luck," Lynne thought in a careless moment and Fancy's chuckles became almost hysterical until she sobered suddenly, looking contrite.

"No, it isn't funny at all really, you probably need a bit of luck. I can't change the rules of course, but if you could have a wish granted, what would it be?"

"No problem," said Lynne. "Having my numbers come up on the lottery would take care of a great many wishes …we could pay off the mortgage or even afford a bigger house. A reliable car, a holiday, a new washing machine – all, or any one of them, would be marvellous! The children are begging for a computer; they could have one each if we won a million. My husband would be able to start his own business. However, there's no point in wishing as you're not in a position to help."

Fancy looked sad and promised that, if ever she fell desperately ill, she'd return and let Lynne nurse her. Lynne was horrified. It might tempt her to hope that Fancy's health would decline rapidly, and that would be wicked! Anyway, she couldn't imagine how she'd cope with a patient who was shorter than her own little finger. "You could sleep in Sally's dolls' house but sponging your forehead with a damp cloth is out of the question!" They were laughing so much, at the inanity of their thoughts, that neither noticed the arrival of Lynne's husband, Jim.

He cast a strange look at her, before he sat, snapping open his newspaper at the sport supplement. "What's so funny on this miserable wet morning? I have to drive through it, while you just sit here enjoying a leisurely breakfast!" His affectionate smile took any sting out of his words and Fancy fluttered her wings in approval. She admired his fair, wavy hair and declared him handsome, but probably short-sighted, as he hadn't noticed her.

Lynne bustled about serving Jim's bacon and eggs. He immediately started eating without being distracted from his paper, which he'd folded and propped against the milk jug. As Lynne put bread in the toaster, she raised her eyebrows at Fancy and shook her head. "No, he isn't rude. Reading's allowed at a breakfast table." She started cooking for Sally and Sammy, the twins, who were squabbling loudly, as usual, in their scramble for possession of the bathroom. Within minutes, they arrived at the kitchen table, still shouting. Without skipping a paragraph, Jim 'shushed' them – then ignored the fact that they ignored him – and it was left to Lynne to restore order. They never disregarded Lynne; unlike their father, she kept her threats as well as her promises.

Lynne had seen Fancy walk over to the teapot during the upheaval. The tea cosy made a soft warm bed for her and she nestled happily in full view. The white flower pattern camouflaged her effectively and their stream of silent communication continued unabated.

Fancy was astonished that Lynne hadn't met any of her kind before – there were many of them about. "Like you, we're not all the same colour," she explained but we haven't a language problem, so we all get along... black, white or polka dotted we have no prejudices."

"How civilised," Lynne thought, "even some of our neighbours hate each other. Yes, you're right," she added as she picked up the reply, "my children do argue a lot, but only in fun. They don't hate each other."

"Your boy is vicious!"

"Sammy? No, he's actually very loving. You're not seeing him at his best."

Fancy eyed Sammy with suspicion, obviously unimpressed.

Jim glanced at his watch and sighed as he straightened his paper and laid it on the table. He was a hard-working architect and unappreciated except by his immediate boss, who took full credit for all his efforts. If only he could afford to set up on his own, Lynne daydreamed. He could work at home …she would be his secretary until he made a name for himself and could put his own ideas into practice.

"I'm really sorry that magic wands have gone out of use," Fancy sounded subdued. "I'd like to help, but I'm unlikely to get sick and my sense of self-preservation is quite high so…"

As she spoke, she flexed her shoulders and the movement caught Sally's eye. "Ooh, look," she cried with delight, "It's a beautiful…"

"Beautiful nothing!" Sammy interrupted, seizing the discarded newspaper. He threw his arm back and, with his full weight, brought the wad down in the direction of the tea cosy. "It's a cabbage white," he yelled, "They eat our food!"

With a scream of horror, Lynne sprang and succeeded in deflecting his aim. After a flash of frozen panic, Fancy spread her wings and flew to the top of a cupboard where she stood trembling, gazing down. Jim had been halfway out of the back door when Sammy shouted and, rain or no rain, Fancy followed, fleeing for her life.

She hovered briefly before escaping and Lynne stared perplexed at what, from several feet away, certainly looked like a common garden butterfly. Her faith in her own mental stability, however, was only briefly shaken and her farewell thoughts followed Fancy ... "Please forgive Sammy. Thank heaven, the rain has almost stopped, you'll be safe now."

The lucent white wings danced back to the open door and Lynne distinctly heard heartfelt cries of gratitude... "You did it... you saved me!"

That night, when the mid-week lottery numbers were about to be announced, Lynne leaned forward eagerly and demanded silence.

"What on earth has got into you?" Jim laughed, "You can't really think we're going to win."

Lynne hugged herself with glee. "Want to bet?" she asked. "I just know we're going to live happily ever after!"

Snip-Snap

Mary was able to speak normally when she woke ...at least, she supposed she could have, if she'd tried, but living alone with no pets, she couldn't be absolutely sure. Only when attempting to answer the telephone, did she find her lips too stiff to move. Her glottal mumbles at first alarmed her daughter, but Alison decided it didn't sound like a real medical emergency and promised, "I'll come straight round after collecting Jenny from school. No problem".

Jenny was six, a 'Mixed Infant' as she called herself, quoting the words carved over the archaic school entrance. They'd visited only yesterday, to ask if Mary had kept any of Alison's toys. If so, Jenny hoped she could borrow them for a special lesson. The imaginative teacher was trying to instil a sense of history, while her pupils were still at an impressionable age – many couldn't imagine their parents as children at play. Alison had warned that Granny wasn't likely to have anything, and was intrigued when her mother admitted to possessing a rag doll from her own childhood. Jenny squealed with excitement and clapped her hands …"Please, please Gran let me take it?"

Mary regretted having mentioned the doll but, unable to withstand her entreaties, she nodded quickly to quieten the child. Under Mary's direction, after climbing the pull-down loft-ladder, Alison opened the creaking lid of an old trunk and lifted out a smaller box. She carried it back to the landing, where her mother waited. As she stepped off the ladder, Mary took it from her with trembling hands and together they went downstairs where Mary unwrapped Winnie.

Alison gasped. "How come I've never seen her before, Mum? She's exquisite, hardly in the 'rag doll' category!

"It was mean of me," Mary smiled, "not handing her on to you, when you were little, but the time never seemed right. She was really special, not like other toys. Then I forgot her, until you were too old for dolls." Even as she made excuses, Mary knew they were half-truths, but now Winnie was safe: not a plaything, an antique! Seeing how lovingly Jenny held Winnie, she was reassured and allowed the child to enfold the doll again in the yellowed tissue paper and return her to the box.

Restraining three-year-old Robin, so that his flailing arms inflicted no damage, Alison allowed an ecstatic Jenny to carry the borrowed doll to the car passenger seat then strapped the children in the rear. Jenny chattered happily throughout the drive. Other children would bring ordinary toys, "But", she added proudly, "My dolly will be best of all!"

Robin, excluded, demanded, "Dolly, Dolly me... Want Dolly, me–ME", as he squirmed and wriggled to reach the box. Frustrated by his mother's refusal to comply and his sister's superior smile he wailed interminably.

When they arrived home he watched, exhausted at last, as Alison released him and carried the object of his desire inside. He followed, saw it placed out of reach, and turned away pretending he didn't care. Understanding his disappointment, his mother hugged him and switched on the television to distract him while she prepared tea.

Disinterested in cartoons, Jenny sat with eyes aglow gazing up at the box. Robin sprawled on the floor, his back to her. What harm could there be, she thought, in just looking? Climbing onto a chair, she tipped the box and raised the lid, unaware that Robin was peeping under his arm.

When he leaped and tried to snatch the treasure Jenny shrieked and the box fell. She grabbed his wrist and twisted his hand from Winnie's delicate face. His little fingers curled and clutched as she rescued the doll – both grimly silent, knowing they'd be in trouble if their mother appeared. Jenny's superior strength prevailed eventually and when Alison returned, Winnie was safely shelved again – undamaged as far as Jenny could see.

Watching the car drive away, Mary had sighed; their visits were so soon over. She was disquieted about relinquishing the doll, even for a day. Seeing it again had evoked memories of her grandmother who'd made it so lovingly during the months of waiting for Mary's arrival. Listening to her daughter giving birth, upstairs, Grandma put the final touch to the face, chain stitches delineating the mouth. As she cut the thread, the baby's first cry rang out. "Snipped it," she told Mary, "just as the doctor snipped *your* little chord… your twinnie, that's what she is!" Mary eventually got her tongue round 'Winnie' and the name stuck but she never forgot its origin.

Winnie was always handled with care.

Unlike other dolls, she was not shared, broken and eventually discarded. In infancy, Mary cuddled her under supervision. Later, she adorned Mary's bed during the day and rested nightly on her bedside table: a comforting presence in darkness: a friendly face every morning. Mary's husband teased her when he discovered the doll with them on their honeymoon but accepted that to his bride it was a symbol, almost a lucky charm. When baby Alison began to toddle, he advised putting Winnie away, knowing how devastated Mary would be if she were damaged. When he died Mary considered retrieving Winnie from the attic, but it had seemed too much trouble and rather silly.

Mary eventually emerged from her reverie with an unusual sense of freedom. For years, agoraphobia had prevented her from going out unescorted, even though she sometimes longed to escape from the house. Was it possible to suffer from claustrophobia at the same time? It seemed ages since she had felt at ease either inside the house or in the garden but, seeing the late afternoon sun casting lace-like patterns of leaves over the lawn, she opened the conservatory door and without hesitation stepped into the fresh cool air. Breathing deeply, strangely calm, Mary walked around the garden several times before sinking to the soft grass. She felt drugged by the scent of roses and overwhelmed by the novelty of enjoying open space. Her house had been like Winnie's box; now they were both free.

When darkness fell, Mary reluctantly went inside. The nightly ritual of locking herself in seemed unimportant and she was soon in bed, falling asleep, dreaming of simple pleasures, long forsaken: shopping alone, walking in the park, or perhaps, even taking the children to the zoo.

Her sudden release from unidentified fears was miraculous … no longer would she be a burden …Alison would be overjoyed.

Alison's daily phone-calls were routine. The last thing she'd expected, having just seen Mary yesterday, was to find her mother in trouble, but she'd be able to return the doll, so was glad of the excuse to visit again. She didn't think her mother was really ill but was anxious to make sure and relieved to see Jenny waiting inside the school gate, clutching the box. Still bursting with excitement Jenny ran to the car as soon as her teacher acknowledged Alison's arrival. Robin's interest in the doll seemed to have waned but it was placed well out of his reach as they drove away listening to Jenny's animated account of the wonderful toys she'd seen.

Mary's initial shock at her plight had passed. She felt fit otherwise. Her mouth would surely get better. It was fortuitous that Winnie would be returned quickly and she'd see the children again …twice in one week! Although unexpected, the doll's imminent homecoming was welcome. Instead of being hidden away she could share her bedroom again – perhaps have a place of honour in the sitting room, to keep her company. When she heard the car arrive, Mary made up the fire and settled down …tea tray, juice and biscuits ready.

Even before Alison's key was out of the lock Jenny rushed in to describe the amazing things she'd seen: a teddy with only one leg and one eye, donkeys, monkeys, an acrobat tumbling...! Alison interrupted laughing, "Give Gran a chance to say hello". Instantly contrite she added, "Oh, mum. I'm sorry! How are you? Can you speak yet?"

"No!" Mary mumbled. "Don't worry. Fine otherwise. Numbness will go soon." She nodded towards the box, indicating where her greater interest lay.

"There," Alison said, lifting Winnie out. Suddenly confused, Alison halted and gasped, "Oh! Good heavens!" A shiny pink thread dribbled from the lips; the tiny chain stitches were unravelling. "How on earth did this happen?" She glared fiercely at Jenny, who stared wide-eyed at Robin, sullenly shrinking far into the depths of the settee.

He scowled at the doll: the cause of his trouble. "Never mind now. I'll fetch a needle to repair it – it'll only take a few minutes."

Leaving Winnie on the chair arm, Alison withdrew, unwilling to meet her mother's eyes.

Mary watched the children, perceiving the guilty aura between them. Alison was right. The damage could be fixed. Neither child should be punished for what must surely have been an accident. She wished she could speak, to comfort them. Seeing only sympathy in her gran's expression Jenny climbed on her lap and resumed her account, heedless of Robin's increasing resentment.

Mary watched him edge towards the doll and

stared anxiously as he fingered the hanging thread. Impeded by Jenny and unable to shout, she couldn't prevent him from pulling it. He grinned when, like magic, a loop in the centre of the mouth disappeared. Another popped up instantly and he gleefully jerked it again. With each tug, a stab of pain shot through Mary's lips. The coincidence was immediately unacceptable and horrific, draining her of strength!

Jenny's weight seemed to have doubled, she could only stare helplessly, but thank God he stopped, looking towards the door.

Robin pondered, glaring at what was left of the rosebud mouth. His mother would notice if the line disappeared, but bruises wouldn't show if he punched the doll's soft, pink legs. His clenched fist crashed down. With a strangled howl, as pain seared her knees, Mary shoved Jenny to the floor and the affronted, screaming child ran for her mother. Robin, aware only of his own pleasure in revenge, laughed aloud. He'd found an even more satisfying way of inflicting untraceable damage.

Alison halted her headlong rush into the room and stared in disbelief. Her mother was slumped over, legs dangling as if disjointed, clutching her head. Blood pouring between her fingers had already soaked the sleeves of her blouse. Terrified, she ran to telephone for help... whatever was amiss, coping with it was totally beyond her.

Robin was happy. The pen he'd found made satisfying plopping noises as he stabbed it through Winnie's thick, coiled hair. Not until his arm tired, did the fabric split. Stuffing burst out and would not go back. When he tried to push it in, more of the soft woolly Kapok spewed forth.

Fibres rose in the warm air making his nose itch …he rubbed his face, scattering the white clumps that clung to his pullover. Then the full magnitude of his crime dawned, driving instantly from his mind all but the inevitable consequences of his recklessness. Shaking with fear, desperately, he sought a solution. Hiding the doll was pointless, it would soon be found; complete destruction was his only way out!

Mary, now barely conscious, saw his gaze rest on the blazing fire and knew what he intended to do even before he raised his arm…

With Jenny crying, clinging to her skirt, Alison rushed back, calling Robin to come out immediately; poor child, how could she have left him alone to witness his grandmother's distress. He was sitting quietly, apparently oblivious to her condition, thank goodness, and she turned to reassure Mary that help was coming.

There would never be a satisfactory explanation of why, how, or what had happened. A smoky haze hung over her mother's chair and a deep layer of ash covered the cushions. Clutching the children, backing slowly from the room, one thought kept hammering through her brain...

However inexplicable, however bizarre, she had to accept the fact. There was no one there.

Mail Ego

"Apart from bills," Flo greeted him brightly," several other things came for you today. Something from an investment broker who knows where you can get at least 15% on all the money you haven't got and, not one, but two real letters!"

Jerry removed his mail from behind the clock where she always propped it, after going through it herself. Ignoring those with windows he glanced at the postmarks on the others. Before he could assimilate their origin, Flo shouted from the kitchen.

"Your niece has a new baby and your brother wants advice – Thelma is threatening to leave him!"

Jerry shoved them back; the details would keep.

Fuming, he went upstairs to change from his suit. He was forty, for God's sake! He didn't need a minder to shield him from bad news!

After fifteen years of marriage it would be nice if, occasionally, he could enjoy the thrill of slitting open envelopes addressed to him. She even saw his birthday cards before he did!

Dinner was ready so, hearing the shower running overhead, Flo read, for the hundredth time since it came in the morning post, the letter he would never see:

'Darling,

Don't be surprised that I should address you this way – it is how I always think of you. My marriage didn't work out and I know now I shouldn't have walked out on you. Can you ever forgive me?

I am back now and hope we can pick up where we left off. If you agree, come to the old kissing gate, where we always used to meet, at nine-o-clock next Thursday night.

I have seen you around and been trying to pluck up courage to speak. You haven't changed a bit. You will recognise me too. I am still slender, blonde and beautiful. Come and see for yourself!

Forever your own Princess.'

Flo gripped the edge of the table. She wanted to scream.

When they were courting, she and Jerry always met at the kissing gate: his Princess, he called her! How many other girls had that special name? How many others had been with him at their private trysting place on the embankment?

Her first resolve, to confront him and assess his reaction to his old flame, weakened as the morning passed. What else could he do but claim disinterest, perhaps throwing it flamboyantly on the fire, but he might still keep the appointment.

Thursday was her bingo night. He sometimes went out for a drink. The children were old enough to be babysitters, themselves, so could be left for an hour or two.

She would never know.

Other men had affairs. How could she be sure Jerry wouldn't be tempted too, by 'slender blonde and beautiful' who was pursuing him so blatantly?

Even if he didn't turn up, there was no guarantee that she wouldn't write to him again or approach him, when he was alone.

During the afternoon, the idea of lying in wait at the assignation spot and confronting her rival, to issue dire threats if she didn't keep her hands and her mind off Jerry, began to appeal ...but it might prove to be an embarrassing, hopeless gesture. Brazen 'Blondie' did not sound like a woman easily frightened.

By the time Jerry's key rattled in the door, she was resolved to sleep on it ...she had three days to come to a decision.

Hearing her husband coming downstairs, Flo pushed the letter into her overall pocket and started serving the evening meal.

Jerry retrieved his post and settled down. Apart from the bare outlines, which he already knew, they contained little of interest. The baby weighed eight pounds and Thelma was fed up because his brother had no ambition. He'd had none when they married ten years ago – what did she expect!

Ten-year-old Adam had his head two feet from the television and hadn't even acknowledged his father's arrival.

"Good evening, son," Jerry said, but had to repeat it, before he succeeded in attracting attention.

"Oh! Hello Dad." Adam turned and saw the letters in Jerry's hand. Just before going back to his favourite program he asserted, "I hope Aunt Thelma's not coming here. I don't like her!"

Before Jerry recovered his powers of speech his thirteen-year-old daughter, Tracy, raced in and threw her arms round him. "Isn't it great? I'm glad it's a baby girl. Is she my second cousin or my first, once removed?"

It was too much! He was so thoroughly churned up, he scarcely touched his meal.

He didn't notice how little Flo ate.

Tuesday passed without incident. On Wednesday evening at Flo's request, having shown him a finger she had cut, when a blunt knife slipped off an onion skin, Jerry spent half an hour sharpening all her kitchen carvers. On Thursday, as soon as she finished washing up, Flo dashed upstairs to change for her night out. She was usually long gone by this time, Jerry reflected.

When she dashed out, she threw him a frantic 'bye, love' and reminded Tracy about her homework. He told her to get going. He wasn't outward bound himself; he would see Tracy didn't forget. "Enjoy yourself," he called after her as she rode off down the drive on her bike.

He watched from the window as she pedalled away in the direction of the Church hall, two miles away. The railway line was five miles in the opposite direction; no doubt she would circle round a back street to keep his nine-o-clock 'date' for him! Her night out was ruined but how could any wife ignore such an ardent declaration of intent? If she pushed hard, she'd make it with fifteen minutes to spare.

He resisted the sudden temptation to follow her in the car – wasn't that the whole point, to teach her a lesson? Well, when she returned abject, after hanging around alone at the edge of a damp field for nothing, he would confess it had been a joke. Perhaps his one and only princess would think twice before interfering again with the Royal Mail!

Just after ten-thirty Flo arrived home. She looked slightly agitated and breathless as she removed her plastic cape. It had rained, she explained. Otherwise she seemed normal, even happy, or relieved perhaps!

"You look pleased with yourself. Did you win?"

he asked.

For a moment she hesitated, then laughed. "Win? Yes, I did. Take your hat off to the big winner!"

"How much," Jerry asked, not believing her for an instant.

Flo hurried through to put the kettle on, avoiding his gaze.

"You mind your own business," she called over her shoulder, "it's nothing to do with you. I'm certainly not paying the telephone bill!"

By the time they went to bed, she still hadn't admitted where she had been. At breakfast Jerry asked again about her big win. She merely shook her head and resolutely chewed toast.

On Friday evening when his train pulled into the station the place was in turmoil. On the 'right of way' across the line, that morning, a body had been found: a middle-aged blonde. She had been stabbed to death sometime last night ...a real beauty they said!

In a blind panic Jerry raced to his car and drove home.

What had he done?

The knives!

What had Flo done!

With all her faults, he adored her ...could his stupid letter have goaded her into murdering a complete stranger?

How could he ever ask?

It had been an inane thing to do anyway. Even without this horrific complication, how could he mention the mythical blonde? Flo would either refuse to believe him or be terribly hurt. He was a fool!

He pulled off the road to be sick.

The children, agog about the murder, were watching the television news. Flo smiled as she read the letter for the last time before flushing it down the loo.

She'd been right to keep it from Jerry; else he might have been at the kissing gate where the dead blonde was found. He would have become involved in the woman's tragic death.

It certainly had been his lucky night!

This year he was going to get the best birthday present he'd ever had from her – the hundred pounds she won last night, at bingo!

Biding Time

Amy paused at the open door, transfixed. Her arms were laden with freshly cut flowers from the garden, but something other than their heavy scent disturbed her senses.

Her ghostly intruders could no longer be ignored. The full, horrific implications of being haunted overcame her ...she had to get away.

Life had been blissful in their little haven for two years after David carried her over the threshold, to collapse in a happy heap on the antiquated Chesterfield.

He'd lamented that they couldn't afford modern furniture of their own, but Amy loved the old pieces – the satin smoothness of polished wood, the grainy strength of tapestry. She was contented in the rented cottage, reluctant to be away from it even for a few hours. David teased her and could have shopped alone, but he insisted that she needed a change of scene.

He planned frequent sightseeing trips and it was on the last one, a year ago, that an accident took his life and shattered hers. ...Instant terror merged with blinding pain.

As a dark veil fell, she'd heard a voice, trembling on the edge of hysteria, "The driver's dead ...the woman's in a bad way!"

Amy had no recollection of the weeks following the tragedy. Her mind blocked out David's funeral and the trauma until she returned home and found a measure of solace in remembering happier times.

In the shade of the cherry tree she re-lived the hours they had relaxed, reading together. She played David's favourite music interminably, never tiring of the images revived – a half-smile touching his mouth during difficult passages or his sigh of appreciation at the end of a moving aria. He'd loved her long hair and brushed it every night. David – gentle, handsome, was as dark as she was fair. She hugged her memories to keep him near, existing trancelike, unable to accept the bitter truth. She was alone.

Before David died, Amy had never hallucinated and was scornful of those who claimed to be psychic ...but things changed. Fleeting shadows on the periphery of her vision eventually became images as clear as her own familiar surroundings, but she was more puzzled than scared.

They were easily dismissed as illusions.

Amy supposed the damage to her head might not yet be completely healed.

The ghostly presences of 'Mr and Mrs Misery' were intriguing – a fascinating distraction from her own unhappiness.

However, she felt a positive dislike grow for the thin, bitter woman who insinuated herself everywhere, arms folded aggressively over her garish apron. Her dull-grey hair was scraped into a tight bun and it was galling to see her cleaning and possessively, lifting, touching things.

She was a *real* misery, sour-faced, always angry with her husband. He was *in* misery, enduring – not rising to – her taunts. It was like watching a mime unfold and Amy became more absorbed in their lives than her own, growing accustomed to finding them already there when she entered a room or went out to enjoy the garden.

When she began to hear them, Amy beguiled herself into acceptance ...faintly echoing voices were wind in the chimney or twittering birds. As if from afar, disjointed sounds drifted, merged and were rendered meaningless. By the time whole sentences, became audible, Amy was inured against traces of fear. She did begin to feel uncomfortable, though, like a voyeur, as the couple bickered more and more. She felt disorientated – an intruder in her own home – but refused to consider flight.

If only the woman had been less of a harridan,

Amy could have derived comfort even from such strange company, but the shrill voice grated on her. Why was this obnoxious woman plaguing her? She could not take much more! Yet, if she left, where would she go? She had no family or close friends, but she would not be driven out!

Then an idea gripped her ...if she could see one ghost, why not another?

Why not David?

Hope consumed Amy. More than ever before, her deep yearning to see her husband tied her tenaciously to their home. She became inured to the intrusion of the loathsome pair.

Terrified that she might miss him, should his return be brief, she barely slept. She was convinced that David would soon be with her, relaxing in the depths of the fireside chair or working at his desk.

As time passed and he didn't appear, Amy began to panic.

Why were the Miseries everywhere and David nowhere? The constant presence of the apparitions, to the point where she was hardly ever alone, made her question her own sanity.

She dreaded the increasingly long glimpses she had, every day, of the awful woman moving things about in her lovely home. Every evening, Amy had the wearisome task of moving things back to their right place. Only when the Miseries faded away was she able to relax in her own, familiar surroundings. Sleepless one night, she could not banish the droning voices:

"... I won't stand for it," the woman shrieked, "You useless lump!"

"Tell me what to do and I'll do it," the poor man muttered.

"If you're not man enough to get rid of her, I will..."

Gradually Amy caught the gist of the woman's complaints, which at least made the situation more interesting. She laughed aloud. He must be having an affair. Who could blame him!

Suddenly, a reason for their haunting occurred to her. The man had murdered his wife! That was usually how people became tied to the earthly plane ...by killing or being killed. The stupid woman harassed him continuously, nostrils flaring – her mouth twisted into a scowl – blind to his mounting resentment. The giant of a man took all the abuse heaped on his head meekly, but Amy often detected smouldering fury in his dark eyes. She saw his fists tightly clenched and his muscular arms flexing as he fought to restrain them.

Amy's resolve to stay was shaken by the realisation that one day she might witness the actual murder, but she regained tranquillity by escaping more often into the garden, caring for the roses that David had planted on special anniversaries. They were so prolific she kept several bowls constantly filled, as he used to do. He'd never expected her to help in the garden but now she tended it lovingly, copying everything she'd seen him do.

Happily unaware that it would be for the last time, Amy selected some blooms to take inside. The sky darkened as she turned to the house and a sense of foreboding overcame her. She was torn between flight and holding her ground.

Amy entered the eerily silent kitchen fearfully, drawn unwillingly to the dim living room.

Could this be the dreaded day?

Would she see the murder or its aftermath?

She tried to turn back, but a force beyond her was in control. From the doorway, Amy saw that they were both there, but not alone. Incredibly, seated between them, someone else was there, staring straight at her.

David?

David at last?

No, it was a woman …and, unlike the couple, this phantasm could see her, too.

It was too much for her – they had won.

How ridiculous she had been, expecting David's spirit to return. If his violent death chained him anywhere, it would be miles away, on that awful crossing. She fled in panic and the flowers fell from her arms, scattering over the floor, bruising their soft petals.

In the lane, Amy lingered uncertainly, depleted, drained of hope, watching the cottage from afar. It looked strangely hostile in the gloom, but where else could she go?

She sank to the ground, oblivious of time and the encircling shadows, painfully coming to terms with her situation. It was dark when Amy finally accepted that she could never return.

She wept. The tears dried on her cheeks in the cool wind as she walked away.

Still in darkness, she reached the deserted railway station. Trains were infrequent and anyone on duty was probably dozing in an office until the milk train came, but she didn't seek company.

She stretched on a waiting room bench, pulling her cardigan around her thin frame. It was one she'd often worn when shopping with David …how odd that she should be wearing it now. It seemed like a good omen when she felt her wallet in the pocket. She suddenly felt a surge of hope. Surely, it was another sign that her prayers would be answered.

Amy felt much more sanguine by the time the cleaning-crew arrived. She lay quietly before going to buy a ticket, until the door burst open to admit a man with a mop and bucket. She would travel over the fatal crossing, perhaps on the very train which…! She stopped herself from dwelling on the image, focusing her thoughts on the present. There were undoubtedly ghosts who could return and if David knew how much she needed him he would let her see him. Perhaps he'd even stay with her!

Someone asked the stranger in the ticket booth where old Bert was. There were titters in the queue when he replied, "Up the line in Lost Property!" It was all so mundane. Amy moved as if in a dream, her thoughts fixed on re-union with David. She found an empty compartment where two men soon joined her. It didn't matter. She shut them out easily – one reading a local paper, the other intent on a crossword puzzle. Her excitement mounted with every mile. After one more stop they would reach the crossing. It would be the first time she had seen it since the catastrophe that destroyed her life and she should be dreading it. Instead, she was serene, experiencing a sense of fulfilment. Confronting and accepting her fate was the only way go on. Hypnotised by the rhythmic clatter of the carriage, she fantasised about seeing David. He would never leave her again; they could go back home together ...with him she could face anything.

The train slowed and the man opposite discarded his newspaper before leaving the compartment. As the train moved on, Amy stared from the window – nearly there, soon, soon. A draught riffled the paper, distracting her and her eyes flicked to a familiar photograph. It was unmistakably the cottage – her cottage! *"HAUNTED"* asserted the headline. Two people stood at the door, looking concerned.

Bewildered, Amy leaned forward and skimmed through the text:

"...The house stood unoccupied for barely a year after being tenanted, but on their return the owners found themselves sharing it with a resident ghost.

A psychic claims to have performed a successful exorcism. The relieved couple, present throughout, describe the experience as bizarre.

During the séance, the room became drenched with fragrance and the hitherto bare floor was afterwards strewn with rose petals. The elated medium admits that she has never before had such a positive experience. She believes the farewell gift of flowers to have been offered as an apology".

The people featured were her hated interlopers!

It was beyond Amy's comprehension – she was numb with shock. As she stared from the train in dismay, the scene unrolled like a surreal film until it reached the crossing ...and there stood David, smiling, and waiting with open arms.

Bert, at the Lost Property Office, accepted the leather wallet. The man handing it in had not seen who left it on the seat. It was empty except for a faded snapshot, which Albert examined intently. He recognised the young couple. "How odd," he murmured, "who could have left this? Had a terrible accident they did, over a year ago. Killed outright, he was. She died on the way to hospital." Bert sighed heavily and explained. "It was a blessing really because she'd never have survived alone ...such a timid little thing – never left the house without him, unless she had to...."

He labelled and pigeonholed the wallet.

It would never be claimed.

The Hunter

His head sagged into the soft mud; liquid oozed slowly around it, blocking the air. The instinct for survival jerked him to consciousness, turned him sideways, and for minutes he lay gasping, trying to recall where he was – and why.

His limbs seemed sapped of strength: heavy, unresponsive to his will. No glimmer of light revealed his surroundings and he feared that he was not outside in the fresh air. The air, in fact, was stale and he began to retch. If only he could drag himself away from the smelly water swilling over him, he might be able to breathe without being sick. Slowly, painfully, he moved to dryer ground and tried to assess his position and his chances of survival.

Coming up against a wall he fancied the air was moving slightly; perhaps if he groped along it, he would find a tunnel – a way out. It seemed like hours before he became convinced that there were only two options. He was apparently on a slight rise. Behind him the water trickled away to disappear down a sheer cliff; ahead, now that his eyes had adjusted to the conditions, he perceived slightly paler reflections in the depths of the water; escape must lie beyond the far wall.

He hated swimming but braced himself for the ordeal and reached a similar cavern to the one he had left. except that the roof opened out to reveal an almost vertical funnel overhead. Going back, deeper into the unknown, was out of the question but, although he was a good climber, he felt daunted at the prospect of clinging to the steeply rising wall above his prison.

If only he could remember what had happened to him since he left home before dawn – decide where he was – he might think of a way out.

Think!

Think, he admonished himself, what could he recall with clarity? The fruitless hour of hunting until faint glimmers of grey day brought colour to the grass and hedgerows: desperation driving him away from his familiar haunts. Yet, looking back from the riverbank to the hill where he lived, the vision had been clear, and he'd not sensed imminent danger.

Yes, he had been out hunting, foraging for food. His community was large, all assets were pooled and there was a good deal of friendly rivalry among the hunters …each preferred working alone and the most successful was lauded, rewarded with admiration and popularity.

He had never known failure and it was his desire to contribute even more to his extended family, that had landed him in this fix.

Unknown territory: the excitement of exploration came back to him now ...the drifting boat bumping against the bushes tempted him to take a ride but he had not intended to go over the falls in it! It had spun, hurtling out of control until it hit a boulder and he was thrown clear. Then what?

He must have blacked out, but how had he got here?

A sudden swirl of water cascaded over him.

It took all his strength to hold his ground and avoid being sucked under the wall again and probably over the cliff. Even worse, the water had not been fresh. The stench was overpowering. Every part of his body stung as if he'd been burned. He couldn't imagine where the liquid fire came from, but he had to get out before it happened again.

As he moved, something heavy bumped against him ...a body!

Dead – or almost: unseen, trying weakly to cling to him but sliding away. The deluge brought more obvious dangers too; a snake-like creature slithered round him before swimming away, leaving him shaking with fear.

He dodged several glassy slabs as they raced by, their sharp edges could have cut him in two!

The sound of more water gurgling towards him spurred him to move faster away from its path and he clambered up onto a slab, firmly wedged on the upward curve of the rough surface.

The surge came and went, leaving dark clumps of stinking vegetable matter in its wake. The gases rising around him would kill him, if the water didn't; there seemed no escape. He guessed he must be trapped in a sewer.

How he had fallen in was irrelevant but, to conquer his growing terror, he tried to analyse his plight and devise an escape.

Increasing visibility confirmed the full horror of his plight but convinced him that some daylight was filtering down, so it must have been night when he first awoke.

His last memory of being thrown from the boat, returned and he suddenly had a visual flash of a fisherman packing up his gear on the riverbank.

The man had not seen him, so he couldn't expect outside help, he must rely on his own wits to survive. At least, in his present position, he was fairly safe, and the fumes were dispersing in the slight downward draught. It would be foolish to risk climbing while water flushed through the pipe, so he resigned himself to a long wait. With the coming of the next night it was reasonable to expect that the frequency of the falls would decrease, allowing him time to reach the top, and, hopefully, safety ...but, even as he began to overcome his initial panic, there was a deafening clang and what little illumination there had been vanished.

Seconds later, violent drumming roared around him, and he rolled in shock as the tunnel shook violently. The lake of water heaved and knocked him over again. When the noise ceased abruptly, and the vibrations died, an unearthly moaning became audible in the stillness.

He imagined hosts of other lost souls haunting this filthy place having perished as, he was sure now, he would himself.

Confirming his worst fears, a noisome tide gurgled up from below, drenching him afresh, leaving stinking shreds tangled around his weakening body.

This was no way for a hunter to die, he gasped and, thinking of his family – his responsibilities – he determined to fight to his last breath.

The fisherman was resting, tired after his early morning start. He enjoyed the weekends: a couple of hours on the riverbank with only birds for company. He seldom saw another soul and even less frequently caught a fish, but today had been unusually satisfying.

He had not only caught two trout but found a rowing boat which he had dragged on shore. If it weren't claimed it might be useful – it would give him something else to do, cleaning it up and giving it a coat of varnish. He'd looked around for oars, but they were lost and there was no sign of an owner although he did fancy he saw a movement in the bushes. He called out but nobody answered so it was probably a squirrel scurrying away.

His wife was less happy than usual. Not being a country lover, she could not appreciate the fascination of fishing. She didn't object to her husband's passing the time that way; she enjoyed the extra few hours in bed, as he happily went off with a pre-packed lunch instead of breakfast. The fact that he didn't seem very good at it was a relief because, if there was one thing she hated it was gutting and boning fish!

Washing his paraphernalia was a regular chore, which she accepted with good grace but today, because of his struggle with some wreck of a boat, everything was twice as muddy, and his jacket even torn. His picnic basket, still open from when he'd fought the elements to get the thing ashore, was filled with mud and insects – she had swilled water through it and upturned it to dry outside – no thanks to him, it wasn't ruined although, as she eyed the slugs and worms swirling down the plughole, she thought she would never eat from it again with any pleasure!

Restraining a shudder as she scraped off the fish scales under the tap, she wished again that her husband had taken up carpentry or stamp collecting!

It was time to cook it for lunch before she finished preparing the trout so, eyeing the grass stains on the jacket, she put the plug in the utility room sink and filled it with water deciding that soaking was the only answer; anyway, it put off dealing with it until tomorrow...

Despite her misgivings, she admitted that the fish was delicious – worth all the trouble, and her husband was well pleased with himself.

He always took a stroll after lunch and decided to return to the river to take another look at the boat. He'd reported finding it, hoping it wouldn't be claimed but wondered if the owner could have been tossed from it, when it came over the weir. He wouldn't rest easy until he'd walked the stretch of bank carefully; he guiltily reflected that perhaps he should have done so, straight away.

Although wearing heavy boots, walking along the bank was not easy. Slipping, sliding and falling sometimes to his knees, he was aware of the mess he was making of his clothing again but there was no point in searching inland, so he persevered. He saw no sign of anyone near the water, or having scrambled out of it, so, with great relief, he returned home in time for tea.

His trousers were so dirty he left them soaking with the jacket.

His wife would not be pleased he thought, as he pushed them under the water and watched dozens of ants float off ...she hated anything 'creepy-crawly' but never mind, they would be dead by tomorrow!

A few dead ants were better than the sleepless night he would have had, worrying about an injured boater, crying for help, unheard.

The atmosphere in the tunnel had worsened. In the blackness, although the water had stopped swirling it sometimes rippled as if something moved stealthily through it. Many times he struck out, sensing a presence nearby, then was even more terrified that the echoes of his own movement were concealing the approach of an attacker.

Every time he began to relax, a scrape or far off screech alerted him. Surely dawn would come soon, but would he know? The light had been suddenly cut off, as if a cover had been clamped over him. Would it be removed just as suddenly? He had no way of knowing, but its removal might herald another cascade of water. The glassy slab was giving off a sickening fishy smell and, anyway, if he didn't start climbing soon it might be too late.

A furry body slowly climbed over him. In the darkness it seemed twice his own size and he froze in terror. Beady eyes glared into his and with all his strength he threw it off and groped his way upwards blindly. The steep, wet pipe afforded little foothold, but he gradually rose away from the threat of immediate attack.

The occasional splashes behind him became more faint and he risked pausing for a rest. He resumed his slow, steady climb and, when noises from above grew audible, he became filled with hope, despite the darkness.

After hours of struggling, he hit something solid overhead. It felt like a huge grid and with joy he pulled himself onto it. His body ached with the concentrated effort and it was some time before he reached up to discover what was above him. If it was a cover, it was far too heavy for him to move it alone. The sounds from above were louder now; he tried to distinguish what they were.

His excitement, when he heard voices, made him shake ...it could mean that his release was imminent. Over his head the cover moved, the pitch darkness was relieved, but water again descended in an almost solid mass. He clung to the grid and waited for the fall to tail off and, as it did, he found he had company; several of his hunting party were clinging near him, most were more dead than alive. Two dead bodies slid past them and they gazed at each other in dumb shock.

The voices above drew nearer and as a thick, yellow slime fell down on the survivors he heard the woman say, "This should kill them all off. I can't stand ants!" His dying, warning scream was wasted; engulfed, disinfected, it echoed down the empty pipe. There was no one there.

Macho Man

Carole looked him over him speculatively ... the macho man who had been dating Jane Glover for nearly a year. No wonder she had kept him under wraps! He was well-built and incredibly attractive.

Now he'd joined the company and was fair game.

Their mutual friend, Gloria, had been throwing herself at him blatantly for a fortnight but, without belittling her, he had resorted to teasing and didn't even come close to asking her for a date.

Carole decided it was time for a more subtle approach. Already, she'd made sure he had noticed her but, whenever they'd been close enough to speak, had avoided eye contact, giving him no encouragement.

She wasn't old-fashioned, but sensed he was. She didn't believe that the man had to make the first move, but he probably did! He must be well aware of her existence by now so drastic measures were called for...

Making sure he saw her 'twist' her ankle, she wailed loudly about not being able to drive herself; he could hardly avoid giving her a lift home and, with her arms clasped tightly round his neck, he practically carried her inside!

No go!

He managed to escape within minutes.

After he left, she stood (sprained ankle remarkably cured) and went to the 'phone. "Hi, Plain Jane! ...Gorgeous Gloria and Crafty Carole have done their worst! You can rest assured – he's above temptation! Don't forget our reward ...let us know when we are to be bridesmaids at the wedding of the year!"

Bugsy 1998

Gerald knew he shouldn't have let his wife anywhere near his computer ...yet, even as the mean thought popped into his head, he knew he was being unjust.

Anyway, he'd supervised her every move as she transferred several images from her new digital camera to the special folder he had created for her, in his desktop publishing program. It was labelled 'Jane', in a section he called 'Albums', and he'd observed anxiously as she saved four fine views of their house.

His own folder, 'Gerald', was subdivided into 'Office' and 'Studio', which contained scanned photographs of his paintings. Well – it should, but he couldn't find them, hence his grief. It was empty. Not one of his oil-paintings was listed.

His friends, harping on about the marvel of 'Windows', had eventually persuaded him that he was falling behind the times so, with trepidation, he had part-exchanged his old word processor for this impressive multi-million-megabyte model.

He was old enough to remember rooms full of

machinery capable of handling only half of one megabyte at a time!

For days, he'd had to steel himself even to switch it on, to peruse the amazing variety of programs that loaded automatically with 'Windows 98'.

Soon, he was able to demonstrate its main features to his wife, who had doubted the wisdom of spending so much of their savings. Now she was keen to use it herself.

For the past week, he had begun to feel confident about putting in items of his own. He had scanned and saved photographs and discovered how easy it was to set up pages, for his writing. The spelling and grammar checks were a joy to use.

Yesterday, however, he'd had his first setback – he'd been unable to find several letters he'd intended to print and send.

He was reluctant to blame the computer.

In spite of his clumsy old fingers, moving files between folders should be simple, but control of the 'mouse' needed practice and he suspected he had accidentally 'dragged & dropped' them into the wrong place. He also blamed his own carelessness when one of his little icons (a shortcut to a virus detector) disappeared from the opening screen.

He loved the array of tiny pictures, which, just by double clicking his mouse button, directly opened any of his favourite programs. So, in spite of minor irritations, he was a proud convert to the new computer age, lamenting that he had not had one during his working life.

Today though, he wondered; had he done the right thing? Was he incompetent – too old to cope with this new technology?

The inexplicable disappearance of his pictures occasioned serious misgivings. Could they have somehow been transferred to Jane's newly created folder? He suddenly remembered that it was possible to locate all the information in the machine by going into 'Explorer', where everything was listed. In theory, it was like any filing system but instead of handling cabinets stacked with paper, the contents could be reached instantly with a magical click of the 'mouse'. Folders opened to reveal sub-folders, in which files were stored – quick to handle and satisfyingly neat. 'Albums' opened at a touch and did indeed reveal his most recent additions, folders for 'Office, 'Studio' and 'Jane', but the mystery deepened.

They were all empty. There was no trace of the missing files. Apart from the fact that Jane would be upset (having deleted the original photographs from her camera), he was angry. His new toy wasn't performing properly, and he felt totally out of his depth.

In desperation, he checked the recycle bin.

Deleted files automatically went into it and, if mistakenly erased, could be restored.

Neither letters nor pictures were there but, to his astonishment, it contained not only the virus scanner 'shortcut' icon but also the whole virus detector program! His stomach churned. He certainly wouldn't have binned *that* deliberately. He dragged it back into operation and restored the icon to the screen before resuming his search for the missing files. He was unwilling to give up. He had, after all, witnessed the photos being saved – seen and admired them. How could he explain their loss to Jane?

His last hope was the section holding Temporary files, which, created by the computer itself, should be filled with transient information. Once the operation was completed, they were useless and could be wiped out. There were sixty-five! Judging by the dates, he saw that most of them related to the downloading from Jane's camera and his own photograph scanning, proving that they had existed. However, they weren't retrievable, so he deleted them and painstakingly ploughed through the few remaining. All but one had the correct suffix, '.tmp' . It was called 'comp.bug'.

Puzzled, Gerald clicked it, not really expecting anything other than garbage, but the screen cleared, and a colourful scene appeared ...his painting of a country lane, one of the first he had saved. An astonishing difference was the presence of a house – *this* house – as depicted in one of Jane's photographs! The nameplate had been altered to "Chez Bugsy" and something about the quality of the reproduction reminded him of an interactive game screen. Slightly bemused, he held the pointer over the bell and pressed the mouse button. A loud ding-dong echoed from his speakers and the door swung open.

By moving the 'mouse' he entered a most attractive room. The comfortable furniture reminded him of an interior design program he'd loaded into the computer a few days ago. An electric fire burned in the fireplace and above it, in a frame he recognised from his collection of clip art, was another of Jane's snaps. With the pointer, he explored. Clicking a bookcase magnified it onto the full screen and the first thing that caught his attention was a box file labelled 'Letters'. Alongside it were others containing, according to the stickers, 'Paintings' and 'Photographs'.

He was almost beyond being surprised when clicking on each revealed most of his lost material. The few absent paintings were blatantly adorning the walls of the room! Gerald thought he was way past the point of incredulity when, without warning, a door on his left opened. Filling the space was an insect. Apart from being fat and brown, it looked like a Mantis as it swayed slowly across the room to sit on a chair.

It stared – watching his jaw drop.

It spoke – a half-smile creasing its small head. "Say something, for goodness sake." When Gerald didn't respond the creature continued. "I thought you'd take longer to find me." Discovering his voice, at last, Gerald gasped something but was interrupted, "You're wasting your breath if you don't use your mike!"

Activating the microphone, Gerald stuttered... "What? I d-d-don't understand. Who are you? Wh-wh-what are you doing here?"

"Bugsy," the thing replied, "and I'll bet you're Gerald. Your name's on the software registration. What d'ya think of my pad?"

"You've stolen my f-files ...you can't stay! G-g-get out!" gasped Gerald.

"Stolen? STOLEN? You might regret calling me a thief." Bugsy re-joined ominously. "You'd better consider your position – and don't even think of deleting me. In the few seconds it would take you to empty the recycle bin I'll have taken half your files with me and the rest will look as if they've been through a shredder."

Not trusting himself to answer, Gerald pressed 'Escape' on the keyboard, clearing the screen temporarily. It was as if the dreadful bug had read his mind. He tried to calm down, taking deep breaths. Perhaps he could gain time by pretending to accept the situation. He opened 'comp.bug' again, hoping it had been a figment of his imagination and that nothing would appear, but the 'thing' was still there, leering.

Trying to smile, Gerald asked, "Would it be asking too much that you put copies of everything back in place? In future I'll back up everything I do, so that you can use of it without inconvenience."

"I don't see why not," said Bugsy, cocking his head disarmingly, "Live and let live, Eh? Switch off and give me ten seconds."

Staring at the blank monitor screen Gerald counted to twenty, to be sure, then booted up the computer again. Using 'Explorer', he found that the letters and pictures were indeed back. The next thing he had to do was figure a way to rid himself of the bug. He double-clicked the recycle icon, hoping for inspiration and saw that the virus detector had been assigned to the bin again! Bugsy was obviously taking no chances.

As a member of the local Computer Club, Gerald knew people who'd had viruses but never had he heard of an actual bug confronting anyone else? If they had, would they have told anyone? No. Like him, they'd fear being laughed at. He considered inviting someone to come and bear witness but, even if the bug spoke, it wouldn't prove that it was acting independently. It could easily be thought that he'd set up the program himself, as a joke, and insisting otherwise would lead people to doubt his sanity.

For the rest of the afternoon Gerald investigated every part of his computer, becoming more familiar with how it worked, searching for a way to destroy his unwelcome lodger. He was glad Jane was spending the day with a friend – she would have been horrified and frightened by the dreadful thing and probably refused to have the equipment in the house.

A glance at the time showed that she would be home in less than half an hour. Every ten minutes or so he had checked up on Bugsy and, more often than not, 'Chez Bugsy' was empty, making him wonder what havoc the beastly thing was creating in his filing system. Whether it really mattered or not he wasn't competent to judge but he decided that, when the moment of destruction came, Bugsy must be at home – preferably snoozing by the fire!

As he searched, he was aware of something relevant that was nagging on the edge of his memory but couldn't bring it into focus. He cast his mind back to his first visit to the club, when he was trying to decide what to buy. Several members had brought their computers in, to have problems solved by other enthusiasts. It was a particularly interesting meeting. He'd hovered nearby, listening and learning. Then, it suddenly came back to him; someone had asked why, when he deleted things, they never went into the Recycle bin. What was the answer?

The memory crystallised as he heard Jane drive into the garage. The man who asked the question had just up-dated from an earlier version of 'Windows'. He was used to using 'File Manager' and had continued to do so. Gerald distinctly remembered the instructor saying that it was silly not to take advantage of the recycling facility as it was easy to delete by mistake ...doing it the old way files were wiped immediately. That was exactly what he wanted – Bugsy's instant demise! He had no idea where to find the setting, but he did as he'd been shown when trying to locate anything. He typed 'File Manager' in the space against 'FIND' and crossed his fingers. A list of twenty-six files popped up, all with little icons. With a cry of delight, he recognised the little filing cabinet against 'winfile.exe' and double clicked as he heard Jane's key in the door.

After locating 'comp.bug' Gerald dragged the window to the right of the screen and, alongside it, he opened the view of Bugsy's sitting room. He held his breath, delighted to see the creature fast asleep. He moved the pointer over to 'comp.bug' to select it, then, warily watching the unconscious bug, he found the 'Delete' button on the keyboard and pressed it firmly. In the instant before it vanished it awoke and the expression of disbelief on its face made Gerald laugh aloud.

"Who's with you," called Jane, from the hallway.

"Nobody, now," Gerald happily informed her. "I've spent hours de-bugging the system."

Jane walked in and looked over his shoulder. "You clever old thing – I'm terribly impressed. It looks as if it's working well." She kissed him on the cheek and hurried off. "Casserole for dinner – dishing up in minutes, so you'd better pack up. You must be tired anyway, if you've been computing all afternoon."

Gerald certainly was tired and his back ached, but he was happy. He moved the pointer to the taskbar and instructed 'Windows' to close. When asked to confirm that he really wanted to shut down, he slid the mouse over the pad until the arrow pointed to 'OK'. He depressed the button but, in the few seconds before the screen went black, a tiny, fat, brown insect squeezed into the picture. It swayed drunkenly upward over the colourful logo, its small head moving from side to side, as it cried pitifully,

"Mama… Mama, where are you?"

Centred on the monitor screen was the message, *"IT IS NOW SAFE TO SWITCH OFF YOUR COMPUTER"*. Gerald switched off feeling slightly sick. Would he ever feel safe again?

Going Down

Drowning?
Is her life flashing before her eyes?
No final curtain?
Her thoughts whirled... Things just cannot end like this... I have too much to live for – it's not fair!

The sisters had never been close. Cissie's mother died when she was eight and her wealthy father re-married. His new wife had appeared very loving at first and Cissie resigned herself to the situation. For almost two years she had been Daddy's princess and had adored him. Being replaced by a queen was bad enough but when, within months, another princess appeared on the scene, life changed.

She was careful to hide her resentment when the baby assumed the centre of attention. Even at her eleventh birthday party, eight-month-old Bella had been the star attraction. Her friends competed to teach her words or playing 'peek-a-boo. Even worse, all the parents, picking them up at the party's end, lingered to admire Bella.

Nobody noticed when Cassie walked away, back to her own room.

Things only got worse in the years that followed. During her teens, she was expected to baby-sit – often into the early hours and her homework suffered, as did her examination results. Bella's mother took care that nothing interfered with her daughter's education and both parents were justly proud of her achievements. With her mother's incredibly good looks and elegance, Bella's future was destined to be a glittering success ...*if she had one.* Cissie pondered, not for the first time in her life, how to solve the problem of Bella. She had always shrugged off the barely formed wish that Bella's luck might change – she regarded herself as being kind and good and would never wish ill on anyone.

As the years passed, her position in life became more mundane than Bella's, in every way, but she avoided dwelling on it by moving away from her hometown. She returned occasionally, to celebrate special occasions – the biggest being Bella's spectacular wedding to a sporting superstar.

His gaze hardly ever left his bride, although the eyes of most females present never left him... He was certainly a 'good catch'! Cassie really wasn't jealous – just resigned to the fact that Bella could have married someone even more famous and heaps more wealthy!

A few weeks later, when she discovered that her father's wedding present to the couple was a luxury villa, Cassie was less sanguine about the situation.

She was working hard to pay off a mortgage on her own flat... She hadn't asked for help and nothing had been volunteered. Did she have to get married before she qualified?

A few months later she was invited to their housewarming party and accepted.

Bella was looking forward to seeing her sister again. It would have been easy for Cassie to resent having her mother replaced and she could have been even more upset when she had to share her father, but no, she was wonderful: always ready to listen and to help, whatever the problem.

Bella was almost embarrassed whenever she had excelled at school or uni' – or was progressively promoted in her job, because Cassie's life in comparison, seemed so unremarkable.

In fact, she also owed her life to Cassie; one thing Bella hadn't excelled in and Cassie did, was swimming. A huge wave had swept Bella out to sea on an out-going tide and, after swimming to catch up with her and hauling her struggling body back to the beach, even Cassie was exhausted. Bella had been in her late teens then and no lightweight!

It would soon be time to meet her train, so Bella took a last tour of inspection and then locked up; Rob was working late so he had booked a table for them this evening and would meet them at the restaurant. When they all returned together, she would enjoy seeing Cassie's reaction to their new home. The sisters would now have lunch in town and spend the afternoon exploring – there were some spectacular views from the cliffs.

Only a few days ago, knowing that Cassie would be at the housewarming, their father had had '*a quiet word*' with her. He was clearly having second thoughts about the wisdom of buying a property for one daughter without any word of warning to the other. "I just want you to know," he assured her, "that when you get married, I will do the same for you." So... Unless she married would she not qualify for his assistance? Perhaps pushing her into marrying would increase the chances of his being a grandfather!! This gave rise to another thought... His wife, they knew, could expect their home to be left to her, but the money was to be split three ways. Bella's husband would inherit their property if anything happened to her, but not the money, *if she died before her father...*

This knowledge churned in her mind throughout the train journey. She'd been tired before it began, having worked overtime for a couple of weeks to earn the right to be away for one. She was exhausted when it ended; noisy, squabbling children and a fretful baby had prevented her from dozing off. Hauling her luggage onto the platform she was relieved to see Bella hurrying towards her... They would no doubt be home soon, and she'd be able to relax – even stretching out on a settee would be bliss.

A few minutes later, as Bella heaved the luggage into the car boot, she described her plan for the rest of the day. After coffee they would stroll along the cliff to show Cassie the wonderful views. After lunch, they would go window shopping and, if Cassie liked the idea, they could visit the local museum. If they wished, depending on the time, they could go for a pre-prandial drink before joining Rob for dinner.

There was no staunching Bella's chatty flow.

She was excited to have Cassie visiting and anxious that she should enjoy every minute. It was clear that any sign of reluctance to do so would upset Bella, so she shrugged her acceptance and followed her out of the carpark.

They did stop for coffee, but Bella couldn't wait to continue her sightseeing tour, so the too-short rest resulted in making Cassie feel even more deprived of sleep. It was after the uphill drag to the cliff top that Cassie started to feel angry. Perhaps Bella was trying to finish *her* off; perhaps she had worked her sums out too!

On the walk down, where the path hugged the rock face and only an inadequate-looking wire fence pretended to offer protection, Cassie was sorely tempted to give in to her violent rage, but the path soon widened, and the sea below rolled more gently against the headland on way to the beach. Cassie stumbled and Bella grabbed her arm. "Don't for goodness sake fall in here – it is really deep – nowhere to climb out!"

Perfect, thought Cassie. A quarter-mile swim to the beach was nothing ...and, before she could change her mind, she stumbled again, grabbing Bella's legs on her way over the edge.

Together they plunged into the water and sank rapidly.

Kicking herself free, Bella started to rise but something held her ankle down at the same moment that she felt her arm tightly gripped.

Cassie was dragging her down too!

Kicking wildly, her lungs almost bursting she looped around Cassie taking masses of seaweed with her, struggling to kick herself free of restraint. Briefly, as her arm was freed, she realised that her foot had smashed into Cassie's head and she hung limply.

Pulling free of the weed, Bella kicked to the

surface with all her strength. After taking a few deep breaths she dived down and did her best to pull her sister free of the trailing weed. It was hopeless. Before her third attempt she noticed that a small crowd had gathered on the path above and several people were using their mobiles – calling for help or taking pictures – it didn't matter, she had to keep trying.

The local newspaper, a few days later, did have some dramatic photos of her leaping out and down again in the waves below and eyewitnesses described her valiant attempts to save her sister.

She relived the minutes on the cliff path over and over, as she swam to the shore. She'd been looking forward to showing Cassie how well she could swim now, thanks to Rob's training – she even had a few cups for winning at local shows.

If she had not been able to swim, would she have drowned too?

Try as she might, she couldn't shake the feeling that it was her fault the weed had become tied to Cassie – and it was her wild kick that had disabled her helpless sister ...but Cassie hadn't been helpless when she stumbled the second time, grabbing her, dragging them both in!

It was speculation best forgotten, better to accept the news report as the truth, the whole truth and nothing but the truth. She could not – would not – accept the alternative.

All Heart

Susan would never forgive herself for becoming romantically involved with her boss. In all innocence she had believed that he was single when he replaced the old manager, who had retired. At the farewell party, Dave had turned up alone and he lived a short distance away from the office in a smart block of flats …at least, she had assumed that he had been living there since joining the firm. Only six weeks ago, when their affair had passed the six-month mark, did she discover that he had a wife. By that time, his wife had suspected, then confirmed his duplicity and had left him.

As soon as Susan realised, she was upset and angry. Even when his divorce came through, she refused, at first, to renew their association but she really did love him.

His persistence, coupled with the fact that she was past her thirtieth birthday, had won the battle with her shame and remorse; she also was an injured party.

When his wife left him, Dave Willis had given up his flat. It had served its purpose, providing a bolthole for him; a place where he could relax and entertain. Now that he was sure Susan had forgiven him, he would buy his soon-to-be-ex-wife's interest in their home and would continue living in it – he had always loved the place. It needed a fair bit of modernising, refurbishing and so on, but Susan would probably enjoy supervising all the improvements.

Susan had been reluctant to give up her job but he had finally convinced her that she would not be comfortable with her old colleagues, being married to the boss – how could they let off steam against him within her hearing? Reluctantly, she agreed and began to look forward to moving into the old house. The chore she was not going to enjoy was walking the dog. It had been the job of the dog-walker since Mrs Willis left but he was only a dachshund – his little legs wouldn't need a daily half-marathon!

On the first of his little walks, all Susan had to do was follow him. He decided when and where they would turn off roads and cross fields and, when they came to an empty bench in the park, he sat – clearly expecting her to do the same. By that time, she was happy to oblige and took out her book to read, enjoying the fresh air for a while.

Later, as she put her book away, preparing to

leave, she heard someone greeting a very excited, tail-wagging dog... "Well, hello Freddy, how nice to see you." Looking up, the woman smiled at Sarah and added, "you must be the new walker – I'm Peggy." Sarah wasn't quite sure whether to nod, or say she might well be Freddy's owner soon, but guessed that Peggy was the previous dog-walker, who didn't seem to mind being usurped.

It seemed rude not to sit down again, at least for a few minutes, so they were soon chatting like old friends.

It had been less than a week since Susan left her office life behind, but it suddenly felt an age since she had relaxed having a good chat. She was soon revealing her life history to the stranger and stopped abruptly when she realised.

Peggy patted her arm sympathetically, saying that she understood and had missed all her friends when she married and moved to another town. Apart from getting out to meet people, she said, she needed the exercise, so walked to town every day either to change library books or do her shopping. "I'll keep an eye open for you and young Freddy here," Peggy smiled happily as she walked away.

While planning their registry-office wedding, Susan settled down into her new role of housekeeper, cook, dog-minder, companion and adoring audience, all to please the man in her life.

She'd never been a dedicated cook and was not surprised when Dave asked her if she could cook something other than stew.

Of course, Peggy was shocked; she commented on what an unfeeling brute he must be. Susan defended him and was happy when Peggy scribbled a list of ingredients on the inside of an old envelope suggesting a few simple, flavoursome dishes, he was sure to enjoy.

Each of these in turn failed to please and Dave was even ill after most of them. When he phoned her from the office between bouts in the restroom, and told her (in an attempt at humour) not to bother making dinner again until she'd taken a cookery course, she was devastated – hurt, but more remorseful at having upset him; she felt so inadequate.

The following week, hoping to redeem herself, Susan decided to start redecorating while he was away on business. She talked it over with Peggy, who had a house-decorator friend who she was sure could paint or paper through the whole house in four days – plenty of time to put up new drapes too, and perhaps replace any worn furniture; there were several second-hand shops where things might be swapped.

After Susan described the aspect of each room, Peggy suggested a colour scheme that could be adapted slightly to suit them all. She declined an invitation to visit the house, saying it would waste valuable time; she needed to put her friend in the picture so that he could shop for materials – and she had another friend who could make the curtains.

Dave was glad to be way for a couple of weeks. He missed Susan, of course, but the few weeks since she moved in with him had not really lived up to his dreams.

If only he had not become bored with her cooking, and hinted as much, she would not have experimented with the exotic stuff he really hated; he had always been allergic to spicy food. He would just have to ask for more 'nursery' food ...his ex's derisory term for everything he liked. He'd asked her to ponder, in his absence, about the redecoration of the house – well, he was thinking more along the lines of restoration than anything modern ...colours and fabrics to show up the quality of the furniture. Most could be classed as antique now – his mother had had such good taste. He was suddenly looking forward to returning and getting on with the job ...and, of course, seeing Susan.

Peggy was in her element. She was a kind-hearted woman and loved caring for people. Susan was so naïve; she had no idea how to deal with this pig of a so-called-man who was taking advantage of her.

He had been exactly the same with his first wife – the poor woman could do nothing right. Coming home late from the office, then complaining that his dinner was less than perfect was not the only example of his mean streak. When he promised her an evening out at the best local restaurant, she spent all day making sure she would look her best. The evening melted away as she waited for him to come home...

His text message at a quarter to eleven, hours after she had cried herself to sleep on the sofa, said that he had been unavoidably delayed. She had tried to smile as she told Peggy what she saw when, on the way upstairs, she looked in the hall mirror ...hair awry, make-up streaked with tears and her new dress crumpled beyond hope.

It was heart-wrenching and a few discreet enquiries informed Peggy that the unavoidable delay had been due to his dining with an office blonde!

She did not regret reporting her findings to his wife, but now she could see that he was being just as self-centred with his wife-to-be. Peggy had no idea whether or not she was the office blonde who had delayed him a few months ago, and really didn't care; no one deserved to be used or misused at the whim of another. Fortunately, she knew enough about him to hit where it would hurt most.

Susan picked up the 'phone on the second ring and although obviously disappointed that it was not Dave, she recognised Peggy's voice and rallied immediately. "It is good of you to take so much trouble Peggy... Oh, I see... Will the dealer really come here to look at the furniture?"

"Yes – and he'll bring catalogues and photos of more modern pieces to replace it... Yes, no problem. Good, we'll be with you in less than twenty minutes."

Peggy smiled, remembering particularly the heavy, Edwardian mahogany, chests of drawers – they were difficult to move without help. Cleaning the bedrooms was almost impossible but he'd been too mean to employ help for her...

It would be easy to convince Susan that the modern furniture would make the bedrooms easier to manage and lighter in appearance. What happened to their relationship after Dave returned and discovered the drastic changes in his home, was irrelevant to Peggy. As far as she was concerned, Susan would be much better off staying single. If not, Peggy would always be beside her, making sure that she stood up for herself and did the right thing. As his first wife she was well placed to know exactly how he should be handled.

Some things you Don't Take to Bed

When she had children of her own, Dorothy understood her mother's insistence that toys cuddled at bedtime should all be soft. No drink at any time should be taken to bed ...a supervised sip from a cup held by someone else might be allowed in certain circumstances. If anyone pretended to be ill, in order to drink without getting up, they were confined to bed for hours, while the rest of the family played a game or watched TV.

It wasn't that her mother was unkind, but the drink rule came about because a cupful of chocolate milk was spilt one night over the whole newly changed bed. The rule against taking marbles to bed was extended to walnuts after a Christmas stocking with nuts in the toe was emptied in their parents bed and, according to their father, a walnut had escaped the thorough search making a hole in his back when he was too tired to notice he'd been lying on it all night.

Ball-point pens were added to the list – crayons had always been banned – and pencils, which had substituted for the pens, were completely out of order after their mother found a half-chewed one that her eight-year-old sister had almost choked on, in her sleep.

Dorothy's twins were usually happy to obey the rules but, for their fourth birthday, they had received a thirty-inch high giraffe from which they refused to be parted.

It was towards the end of the day, when the party guests were long gone, that their favourite uncle popped in, to hand over his birthday gift, on his way home from his office.

The twins had already become familiar and bored with the new presents they had received and, with little argument, were wearily on their way to bed when the doorbell rang.

Favourite uncle's gift had to be opened immediately, of course, and the tired twins became raging whirlwinds of excitement when they unwrapped the huge parcel he dropped to the floor in front of them. There were two things in it but only one immediately appealed to them both. There was nothing wrong with the giraffe, but it was certainly not a cuddly bedtime toy and Dorothy, after her brother had left, did her best to take it away from them. Neither of the twins could be persuaded to release his hold and each was determined to take it to bed.

Daddy succeeded in calming them, but both boys held onto a leg each and refused to part with it. The abandoned stork, equally tall, lay unwanted, only half-unwrapped.

Eventually, they had both been bathed and were ready, "But that thing is metal, with lethally sharp bits," Dorothy moaned, "a most unsuitable toy – what on earth possessed him to buy it! Neither of them can sleep with it!"

Her husband tried to calm her... "Let's just leave them where they are and when they fall asleep, we can hide it somewhere and carry them upstairs."

It sounded like a good idea rather than upsetting them again so, after checking that the twins were still staring each other out, they got back to clearing and restoring order to their home.

The exhausted infants pretended to adopt an aloof attitude towards each other, but when their parents retired to the kitchen to plan a solution, they tugged the giraffe upstairs together. Without speaking, they maneuvered the unwieldy animal into their room and, still clutching their treasure, managed to climb into bed and eventually fall asleep.

Their parents were astonished to discover the living room empty and they crept up together to find the two little combatants fast asleep. The proud parents stared in astonishment... "I'll go and get the camera," her husband mouthed to Dorothy as she took in the scene, her eyes moist.

When the boys awoke in the morning, they saw the two animals standing together on their windowsill. Neither spoke or tried to touch the object they'd both desired so much, the night before.

Over breakfast, their mother explained that Graffy and Storky had missed each other and were happier standing together – just like the twins always were. The boys accepted the situation and Giraffes were added to the list of forbidden things at bedtime.

It was not until they were many years older that Dorothy showed them the photograph taken that night. They lay in their own beds – arms stretched out sideways with each little hand clutching a leg and, between them, the giraffe hung upside down, its nose supporting its weight on the floor. The picture was worth all the tantrums and upset – certainly one for the family album.

A Shaggy Dog Story

Molly picked up Pooch and cuddled him, glaring at her husband as she whispered gently into her pet's ear. "Take no notice of him, my darling," she soothed the shaking animal. "If anyone leaves it will be him. I will never send you away."

"Why don't you both go – I'm sick of the pair of you!" Pulling himself together, he realised he had gone too far and spluttered... "No, no, I didn't mean that ...but he darted under my feet and I nearly went flying. My folders *did* – look at the mess – papers everywhere – it'll take hours to sort them all out again."

Molly was well aware how much Bert hated her darling Poochie.

There was no doubt that her little woolly-haired darling was a messy eater, which led to most of his problems. He had never liked eating out of his dish and, if she took her eyes off him after filling it, he would carry bits away to eat in comfort, stretched out on any one of a dozen valuable carpets.

On one memorable morning, Poochie having

managed to climb into their bed under cover of darkness, Gerald woke to find a greasy half-eaten bone on his chest.

Without the dressing-table stool, Poochie could no longer attain the dizzy heights of the bed, via several other pieces of furniture, but that had not stopped him trying. En-route that day, he had broken a photo frame and tipped over a perfume bottle, which then leaked and spoiled a polished surface. Gerald had never forgiven or forgotten.

Molly scolded Poochie who, being quite clever really, looked chastened. Ears back, eyes cast down, he snuggled his forehead into her cheek before licking her chin, hesitantly. She laughed, put him down in his basket and patted his head before going to help Gerald with his scattered files.

To her relief it did not take long, but Gerald was adamant about Poochie being the bane of his life and now actually a death threat. "I could have fallen and cracked my head open, or had a heart attack, the dratted dog dodging under my feet like that. The sooner he goes the better!"

As she left his study, she heard him still muttering, *"...neither use nor ornament!"*

A week later they were too busy all day to argue much about Poochie's bad habits, as they were attending an official dinner that night. Gerald was president of his local Philatelic club and a special guest from the Royal London Society was coming to talk to them.

Gerald was naturally on edge before the event, anxious that their guest should be met in good time and approve of the venue, as he had been booked into the hotel for the night, rather than have to leave early to catch a train. Everything did go well.

Molly and Gerald, together with a few committee members, joined their guest for a farewell drink at the bar before he retired to his room. They had lingered to enjoy the customary one or two for the road, before saying goodnight to their friends, and it was well after two in the morning when they arrived home to find that they had been burgled.

Their house was as empty as if they had planned to move out. The burglars, knowing they had all the time in the world, had apparently taken all the contents in whatever contained them.

Although devastated, Molly rushed through the empty rooms calling for Poochie. Following her, Gerald was howling his anger; *why hadn't the useless tyke scared them off?*

The police came within twenty minutes and while waiting for a forensic team to arrive they noted, as well as they could, the articles stolen.

Gerald was almost in tears, trying to make the constables understand that what the map-chest contained could not be described merely as stamps... It was a valuable collection, probably worth more than all the furniture put together.

The two young men struggled to keep track of what Molly was listing, between continually interrupting herself to comfort the dog.

"For God's sake, Mo," Gerald snapped, "put the damn dog down and concentrate."

"Was the animal here when the intruders broke in?" PC Blake asked. When they both nodded, he said he would ask the vet to examine it in case it had attacked them; there might be traces on him. Gerald was impressed but shook his head despairingly as he slid gently down the wall to sit on the bare floor.

At the police station, much later in the morning, they were given little hope of finding the villains who had obviously used a large removal van to cart everything away. The event they attended had been widely advertised so, as the President, his absence from home would have been no secret and they most likely watched to make sure his wife left with him.

Allowing that the van could have been at their property within minutes of their leaving, the robbers had a good seven hours to load it and unload anywhere within fifty miles.

If only they had a single clue to follow, said the Detective Sergeant, they might stand a chance of finding everything intact before the load was dispersed, but they had nothing. There had been blood around the dog's mouth, but it was from the mutton bone he had presumably enjoyed while their possessions were being carried out – as Gerald pointed out bitterly to his wife.

Gerald and Molly had always enjoyed their privacy, but nosey neighbours would have been a blessing now.

Poochie, having endured the vet's slow and scrupulous examination for too long, as he left them in no doubt, was glad to be heading home and he strained against the pull of his lead. There was too much traffic to allow him his freedom on the main road, so they decided to take a short cut through the industrial estate, where he could roam safely.

They passed many lorries being loaded and others standing empty and, every time, they couldn't help staring, wondering if one of them had carried away their home. They gave each other sheepish headshakes, knowing without words what they were thinking. Passing a row of several empty vehicles, Poochie suddenly gave a loud yelp and started jumping up and down in a frantic effort to climb inside one.

With a grunt of annoyance and muttering something about taking care not to break his stupid neck when he jumped out, *because he wasn't waiting for him,* Gerald lifted Pooch and almost threw him in. Then he noticed it wasn't quite empty. A small white rug lay in a far corner and the dog was dragging it out.

As it unfurled Pooch jumped on it, triumphantly seizing a trophy, and trotted back, wagging his tail.

Gerald took one look at the bloody bone he proudly carried and took out his mobile 'phone.

As they waited for the police to answer, for the first time ever, he patted Poochie on the head and said, "Good boy," and Molly burst into tears.

Amazing Grace

Grace was relaxing after having put her ten-month old baby back into his cot, already half asleep. Her husband never came home for lunch during the week and most of her household chores were done, so she could watch TV with her feet up. Although happy, reading and having time to chat with friends on Facebook, she felt guilty enjoying herself so much while her husband worked hard, long hours. When they could afford to, they would move nearer to his office. In the meantime, Geoff teased her, saying it was because she was so well organised that she had free time – she deserved it.

Grace was happy to be at home – everything she loved was in it. When she needed to shop, she pushed baby Sam out in his pram for some fresh air. There was a supermarket quite near, separated from their block of flats by only a small park, where she could sit and read if the weather was good.

She had almost drifted off to sleep when the doorbell rang. It startled her because people normally buzzed to be allowed into the building before coming up to the third floor. Peeping out of the spyhole she saw a man she vaguely recognised who looked agitated, so she opened the door with the chain on, in order to speak to him. "I hope you remember me," he said urgently, "because I have a huge favour to ask…"

Without waiting for her to reply, he reminded her that within a day of her own baby being born, his wife had had her baby at the same hospital. Grace did remember and smiled, taking the chain off and inviting him inside. The man was shaking and didn't move beyond the entrance. Grace remembered that he was in the Merchant Navy and was away a lot. He said he had to get back to base straight away but his wife had had an accident and was in a coma.

"She was nearly killed in a traffic accident last night, and our baby is in the flat alone …I can't cope. Could you please come with me and bring him back here? And could you please, please look after him for a day or two?"

Grace was staggered. She had heard police sirens late last night and seen a crowd of watchers across the road, but had not realised it was so serious. She hadn't seen anything much of his wife since they came home with their new babies, but Grace knew that they lived opposite. "Of course," she said instinctively and, after checking that Sammy was still asleep, she grabbed her keys and followed the shaking husband to the lift.

It was a busy road but, once across, it was only minutes before they entered his flat. Everything inside was fairly tidy and Joe – *she suddenly remembered his name* – took her to see his son. Adam was beginning to stir and Joe suggested that there might be a ready-mixed bottle in the fridge. The kitchen was clean but there was powdered milk spilled over the table and floor, and the empty tin was in the sink. Grace realised that the woman – *was her name Josie?* – must have been hurrying to the supermarket when she was hit ...poor girl! Grace was glad to be of help.

Joe thrust the keys at her and suggested that she or her husband could return later to collect whatever else Adam needed. "Don't worry," she assured him, lifting the baby from the cot, "I have food and nappies to spare, so we won't need to come back. Go to your wife now and hopefully she will wake up soon." To her astonishment he hadn't waited for her to lock up. She heard his voice echo along the corridor...

"Must go... Can't stay any longer... Have to get back... Sorry ...Thankyou..."

A few days later, comfortably settled into her new routine; Grace began to worry about the absence of news from Adam's father. Maybe his mother was no better – perhaps still in a coma. She had thought about ringing the hospital but didn't even know the patient's name – or which hospital Josie was in. She had quickly become accustomed to having two babies to love and care for, two beautiful boys. When Adam's mother returned, they must see more of each other... It would be lovely. Geoff was also glad that they were able to help someone in an emergency and knew Grace could cope. She, in turn, didn't want to burden him so kept her worries to herself.

Grace's concern deepened when two weeks passed without any news of Josie and, although startled, it was a relief when she received a visit from the police who were knocking on everyone's door making enquiries on behalf of the hospital. The young policewoman told her that an unidentified coma patient who was showing signs of recovery was worrying about her baby being alone. They had no idea where she lived but were anxious to discover if the baby really existed.

"Her handbag was searched but there were no house keys and nothing to identify her at all. If someone at the scene took them, knowing where she lived, anything might have happened – things stolen – even the baby if there was one," the young woman explained, showing her a photograph, in the hope that the patient would be recognised. Grace was too mesmerised by the story to interrupt. How could they not know who she was?

At last Grace came to her senses and invited them in. "Does her husband know she is beginning to come out of the coma? He came to see me and told me about her accident… Didn't the hospital have their name and address from him?" The fact that Grace was able to show them the baby, and the key Joe left with her, convinced them that she was telling the truth. Grace mentioned the milk powder spill and they agreed that, when hit by the car, Josie must have been hurrying to replace it before the store shut at llpm. After making sure that the baby was being cared for and taking possession of the key, they assured her that they would soon be in touch with her again. It was funny really because, at the point of walking off, they had to ask her exactly where they would find the door it fitted!

Everything ended happily. Grace's mother came to keep an eye on the babies every day while she visited Josie. She spoke for hours to Josie about Adam and sometimes had some response but when she spoke about Joe, the nurse asked her to stop because the patient showed signs of distress.

Months later, when Josie had completely recovered, they met several times a week and became firm friends. Grace had to be careful what she said about Joe. Apparently, he had died months ago, in a collision at sea. The police assumed that Grace had mistaken a family friend for the husband. His reluctance to return was put down to embarrassment – not reporting it officially, or not taking care of the baby himself.

Grace alone knew that she had made no mistake and was happy. She had always suspected that she was psychic.

Sorely Tried

Audrey stared at the kitchen sink. It was full of beans and she really hadn't got time tonight to deal with veggies from the garden. What on earth had possessed him, bringing them in now?

She cast her mind back and tried to remember their conversation before Bernard went out about two hours ago. His throwaway words, as he drove away, had puzzled her ...something about taking care of that when he got back. She'd had no idea what he meant at the time, but two things had become clear. He'd been talking about picking the beans and been home long enough to change, because he would not have been gardening in his suit and good shoes. She could hear him upstairs, obviously cleaning himself up again, to change back into his suit!

She was angry with him. All this messing about was making them late! He wasn't usually so silly – so what had she said to make him even think of harvesting beans? Laundry – yes, laundry had been on her mind... That was it! She had suggested he should bring his gardening *jeans* in from the shed, to be laundered... *Put them in the sink* she had said!

She did sympathise with his growing deafness but, really, they were going out for dinner! He should have known they wouldn't need vegetables tonight. It was ridiculous, doing it now – they could have gone straight out and been on time! Instead, here she was, standing about, kicking her heels. She agonised... *Our friends will be wondering where we are!*

When he came down, a little breathless, but looking his usual smart self, he asked if she had been into the kitchen...

"Yes, I saw the beans." She hesitated and, resisting the temptation to look at the clock, said, "It was good of you pick them so quickly dear – I will be able to deal with them first thing in the morning." His happy smile was more than enough reward for having swallowed her sour words. She really would try to do it more often.

A Dog's Life

Stretched at full length on the bed, he sighed. He was hungry and, until *She* woke up and went downstairs, there would be no breakfast...

Actually, he wasn't supposed to have breakfast, but there was usually a tasty morsel or two, carelessly dropped by the children (*when he bumped into their legs under the table*) or left overs scraped into the waste bin. "There is something wrong with this bin," *She* keeps complaining, "It's always falling over." Luckily for me, the one we call Daddy never takes any notice.

I remember the good old days. when all days were the same, but now some are called school days and we must all get up earlier. Actually, this suits me because, not only do I get snacks, I get to ride out in the car.

Even when there was only one child to drop off, we had to take both and, at first, the other cried all the way home, but it soon realised how much fun we could have together, on our own.

On the second school day, we were not allowed to play in the garden. Never again, *She* said, until the hose was repaired – and put out of reach – and all the muddy soil was returned to the vegetable patch.

In addition, the fishpond had to be fenced off.

Daddy was not pleased with us and, for days, I wasn't even allowed into the muddy back garden on my own. I had to use the one at the front, which upset me... It is overlooked in every direction!

I do like riding in the car, but I never put my head out of the window. I'm far too busy clearing up tasty titbits from the mats

When we get home, I race around checking every room before the vacuum-cleaner arrives. The other day, I managed to drag a biscuit packet from underneath the coffee table. The biscuits were worth it, even though it was a bit of a struggle. The cardboard bit was trapped under one of the legs – but did *She* thank me?

No – just because it tipped over and the flowers fell off!

I was the one that got wet, but *I* didn't complain.

She was angry with me and pushed me outside to dry off, but I still love her.

Things have changed now that both boys go to school. Daddy takes them there on his way to work so that *She* doesn't have to get up early. Daddy doesn't cook things, but we are all happy with toast or cereal so it doesn't matter, particularly because the boys are always in a rush and very happy to drop the crusts for me (*when Daddy is hiding behind his newspaper*).

I am never allowed to share her bed, when they are both in it; mine is on the landing near the boys' room but theirs is more comfortable. After they all leave, *She* doesn't seem to mind my sleeping near her feet. It is safer than being anywhere near her arms ...she once flung one out and clouted me – I had earache for days.

When *She* decides to get up, I'm sent downstairs, so there isn't much to do other than look out of the windows, until she comes down.

The front window has the best view and some people wave to me as they pass by.

I like them.

I don't like cats because they stand and make faces at me, knowing I can't get at them. Barking doesn't do any good, but it does do something... *She* comes rushing downstairs thinking there is somebody calling (*so guess what I do if she is taking too long to get dressed*)!

She puts the television on while she has coffee, but there's no point in expecting her to drop any of her breakfast, so I stare at the screen, because sometimes I see things that look a bit like me. They are called dogs, so I must be one. They have more interesting lives than I do. Some pull people about on leads to guide them and some go out with policemen, to chase people. I'm not allowed to chase anything, especially not cars.

She loves coffee and has even named some of her mornings after it. On these coffee mornings her friends come to drink it with her. Most of them make a fuss of me. They share their biscuits or cake and we all have a good time, but when anyone brings a baby I'm shut out of the room. I'm not sure why. The only time I went near one I did my best to clean up its hands *and* its sticky face. After they've all gone, *She* is quite glad to put her feet up and watch me cleaning up their crumbs.

The afternoons pass quite pleasantly, sitting together on the settee half-watching television while *She* does things with her lap-top; she says it's working, but never stops hitting it; no wonder it doesn't do anything useful. *She* just keeps staring at it, which is annoying, ignoring me until we have to go to collect the boys. At least I know that it will soon be my favourite time of the day... When we get back home, I will have my dinner – real food!

They rarely go out at night, so I settle down on somebody's lap until bedtime. Just as I am really tired and warm, longing to crawl under the blankets in my basket, I am unceremoniously pushed out into the garden and told to 'spend a penny' whatever that means... What a life! They don't do that to the boys!

Soon after I became one of the family, when I

was very little, I made it quite clear that I did not like being in the house alone.

The neighbours very kindly explained to them how unhappy I'd been for the whole time they were absent. The houses weren't all that close together, but I have always had an excellent bark – loud and clear, someone said – and my howls would put any banshee to shame. It made me very proud, hearing that; (*I must find one and listen to it one day*).

Because we don't like being parted, *She* doesn't go out without me during the day but she never takes me inside shops. I have to wait, tied up outside until she has finished. Sometimes I think I'd be better-off being left at home, but it's too late to tell them that. If only I had kept my mouth shut in the beginning, I could have been cosy and contented on the settee – especially if they left the television on.

Just a minute, here comes someone pulling another me, on a lead… If they are going to stay outside too, we could have a chat – get to know each other – be friends! Yes, they are waiting, but so far away! I try, but I can't reach them …and now *She* is coming out and we will be parted… No, our people are talking quietly to each other. They keep looking at both of us and nodding…

They suddenly smile and shake hands and to my astonishment *She* is untying me and handing my lead over. Bending down to hug me *She* is telling me not to worry, "It will only be for a few days, just enjoy your holiday and be good – very, very good."

The one holding both our leads is patting my head, saying, "Come here and meet my little princess. We are looking forward to welcoming you to the family."

Wow, I'm speechless! Looking at Princess I am overcome by waves of inexplicable excitement. I'm still not sure what's happening, but a dog's life isn't so bad after all.

Kids!

Lucy replaced the 'phone on the cradle and hurried back to the kitchen; the stew would be boiling, by now, and she had yet to add salt. She loved talking to her daughter and hearing about all the clever things her grandchildren were doing, but why did Tracey always call before meals, rather than after. Washing up after could always wait but cooking them couldn't! Lowering the gas flame and stirring in the salt, Lucy went to the dining room to set the table and was surprised to find her ninety-five-year-old mother already putting out the mats.

It was on the tip of her tongue to thank her, when she spoke. "The stew is lovely, but you forgot the salt dear." *Oh no...! Yes – her mother had salted the stew!* "...I saw that you were on the hall 'phone, so I did it for you, to help." *Lucy was furious...*

"You really shouldn't have done that," she shouted, "– I hadn't forgotten – Tracey rang me just as I was about to finish seasoning it..." She realised that her mother hadn't heard what she'd said – she'd probably forgotten to put her hearing aid in again, so she raised her voice… "You have ruined it – why do you always interfere with my cooking?"

"Yes. I know you weren't looking dear – that's why I told you… it wouldn't have been a good idea to salt it twice, would it?" She smiled serenely and asked about Tracey, hoping she and the children were all well.

Lucy sighed heavily, thanked her and returned to the kitchen, where she peeled two more large potatoes, sliced them thinly and added them to the stew. That should absorb some of the excess salt!

It would be a much bigger meal than she'd planned but better that, than upsetting her mother who – she knew – would never stop looking out for her, never quite believing that she had grown up.

Inquisition

Time to 'run the gauntlet' again...

Her nosy neighbour was weeding her front garden, as usual, when Jane arrived home from wherever she had spent a few hours. As if Mrs Parker *(well named)* was worried about her and needed to be sure that she was safely back home.

"Hello Mrs Mills! Another driving lesson today? How are you getting on?"

Jane muttered something about being tested soon and Mrs Parker looked happy. "Wonderful! Your husband will be so pleased when you can help with the driving... I expect he'll be buying you a nice little car of your own; ferrying the children to and fro' on schooldays takes him out of his way for work, doesn't it?"

Jane was still only halfway to her front door, when Mrs Parker stepped nearer to the low hedge that separated their properties. "Your friend – the one with the red hair – came while you were out. I didn't come out to speak to her, but she looked worried, so I expect you will want to ring her."

Jane fumed, not being able to bring herself to

comment for fear of saying too much...

"Although ringing people has gone out of fashion these days, I think. It's all texting and Facebook these days ...I don't understand any of it!"

Edging along the path, at last Jane reached the front door. All she trusted herself to say, as she pushed her key into the lock, was, "Thank you, I must hurry to make tea now. The children will be home soon and they are always hungry."

When Jane walked back from the local shops and library the following day, she was childishly pleased to be able to catch the gate before it clanged shut, dodging into the house before her neighbour had time to move from her window to come outside.

She had no occasion to go out again until two days later. Everything she ordered had been delivered but she'd forgotten to include toothpaste – the only thing her husband had wanted!

She left the house as quickly as she could, to go shopping again, careful not to slam door or gate or attract attention. Even so, she was still surprised when she managed to return without being trapped; Mrs Parker was rarely away from her window but had not pounced for days.

For some reason, Jane started to worry.

It was well into the following afternoon before Jane decided to risk being seen.

She wandered down to the gate and looked up

and down the road, pretending to be waiting for her red-headed friend. As she'd expected, she heard her neighbour's front door open and footsteps approached, but she didn't attempt to greet her – no point in encouraging the woman!

"Good afternoon. Are you Mrs Mills?"

The voice was that of a stranger and Jane turned to see a young woman in uniform – apparently a nurse.

Once assured that Jane was indeed Mrs Mills, the woman hastened to reach the pavement to shake her hand, a beaming smile on her face.

"Falling is no joke at any age but you will be pleased to hear that the patient's bruises are fading and she is out of bed now, able to get downstairs to use a walking frame... She is lucky to live next door to caring people. She never stops talking about you and the children – and I hear that you will soon be driving your own car. She seemed quite excited telling me all about it – I expect you'll be able to take her out sometimes."

Jane was stupefied, not sure how to respond. "Yes," she managed to splutter, at last, "She has always been interested in my family."

Before walking to her car, the nurse said, "Having absolutely no family of her own, then it isn't surprising. I must say how good it is to see neighbours getting on so well. It is very generous of you to include her in your life as you do." With a final wave, the young nurse drove away.

Consumed with shame, Jane walked back inside. Having baked earlier in the day she assembled a selection of dainty sandwiches, an apple pie and a couple of cakes on a tray.

When she paid Mrs Parker a visit, in a few minutes, she would invite her to come to meet the family properly on Sunday... It was the least she could do, and it was already a relief knowing that she would no longer feel threatened.

Actually, she might have found a new friend.

A Good Chat

As always, the park was quiet at this time of day.

He passed a few toddlers at play, watched by their mothers or nursemaids, and a few elderly ladies, feeding the birds: no noisy teenagers to disrupt the peace, thank goodness.

Cyril looked across to the bench where he and Vernon often met for a quiet chat. It was never by appointment, at a specific time, but they both turned up at the bench several times a week to enjoy the fresh air and the company of a like-minded friend. He saw that Vernon had already arrived and strode happily across to join him. "So, how are you today, my man?"

"It was hot yesterday," said Vernon, "My wife doesn't like it hot."

"The traffic is heavy, and I was held up at every light on the way here," said Cyril, dusting off the bench with his handkerchief before sitting down.

"She sunburns very quickly," Vernon sighed, "even when she smothers herself in sun-blocker."

"I was out of sorts yesterday but I'm fine

today," Cyril informed him. "My daughter got some medicine for me over the counter."

"I expect we'll go on holiday with our daughter again – spending most of the time baby-sitting..." Vernon frowned; his sigh was almost a groan this time.

Cyril sighed too. "My wife wanted me to see the doctor, but unless you go to 'Emergency' you have to wait days for an appointment."

"So, anyway, we never go away for holidays in the summer," said Vernon. "I would really like to have a holiday in Spain,"

"Anyway, the stuff she bought seems to have worked." Cyril smiled happily, as Vernon continued...

"Friends who have moved to live on the Costa Blanca are always asking us why we don't visit them."

Cyril offered to scribble down the name of the magic remedy... "Have you something I could write it on, and a pen, of course?"

Vernon frowned. "They have a pool and everything, but my wife says they must need it with all that sun." His frustration was evident... "They get temperatures of well over thirty centigrade, you know."

Cyril was just about to speak when his mobile rang. After taking the call he stood and excused himself... "Well – oh dear! I have to go. My son needs a lift. I really am sorry – I was enjoying our little chat."

"So was I," said Vernon. "Never mind – see you again soon."

They waved goodbye, each looking forward to the pleasure of once again being able to relax – talking, frankly, with an old friend.

Last Straw

What to do...?

"Who could have dreamed that every individual in the whole world could be suddenly under threat of death from a previously unknown virus for which there is no known cure? It's a nightmare – it has all happened so quickly. No sooner had we heard of its existence than it was breaking out everywhere on the planet! The only way to be safe – or not pass it on to others, is isolation."

Lisa's mother, Martha, was in a nursing home and astonished to receive her telephone call. She and most other residents hadn't understood why their usual visitors had stopped coming. When Lisa explained and said she was also staying away from the rest of their family, not yet being sure that she could stay virus-free, Martha told her not to worry, *"worse things happened at sea"!*

The risk of passing it on to her loved ones frightened her even more than catching it! She was still mourning the death of her husband but now, knowing how this lockdown would have been a nightmare for him, she reflected with a sad sigh, that her situation could have been a lot worse!

She had been distracted by her train of thought and was jolted back when Martha told her that her closest friend in the Home was not at all well. She'd promised to keep her company in front of the TV, "...and the quiz show must have started by now, so I have to dash – sorry!"

The phone went dead... Slamming it back onto the cradle she couldn't help feeling angry and frustrated... *We'll all end up dead at this rate*!

Four weeks into the pandemic, Lisa settled into a regime. A kind neighbour, Elsie, shopped for her and left the goods in her porch, together with the bill so that the money could be transferred between bank accounts. Several heavier items were available on-line, so she rarely left the house.

Her divorced brother-in-law still rang her up so often that she suspected he might have ulterior motives! All in all, she enjoyed her quiet life now. Her daughter was happily married, living abroad and wrote lovely long letters. Now, these were supported by video calls on their I-pads!

The long days in isolation had enabled her to catch up on all the reading she'd accumulated: apart from library books there was a stack of half-read magazines. Some were still in their plastic covers, and she had meant to cancel them... Now, she had time to try some of the recipes that had appealed to her, and suddenly felt the urge to bake. It was several hours later, eyeing the fruits of her labour, that she wondered what she could do with so many cakes and pies! Watching them cooling in their trays, she suddenly had the answer – she could give most of them to her neighbours.

As they had cooled and were still untouched, she wore one of the thin rubber gloves – an unused gift received ages ago (having professed a desire to redecorate) and packed the fruits of her labour into plastic bags – thank goodness she had a plentiful supply! Her next move was to ring Elsie, who agreed to collect them from the porch immediately, and was delighted when Lisa said that she could give them to people who were most in need.

There were so many rules to obey now, to prevent the contagion spreading; no touching, keeping yards away from people, wearing facemasks in case you have it yourself (as yet undiscovered) so that you don't infect anyone else...! It was a nightmare. Washing hands regularly was no hardship ... it was a lifelong habit always to assume that they were unclean before starting anything new!

A noise in the street penetrated her reverie

and drew her to the window… Unbelievable! For as far as she could see, balconies were full of people shouting and clapping! She'd heard on TV that it was being done to thank all the care-workers and hospitals for their sterling devotion to duty. Although equally grateful, she held back from joining in – it wasn't in her nature to display her emotions publicly.

The news on TV covered little else other than the spread of the virus. After several attempts to find entertainment by switching stations she gave up. There was very little on – and much as she admired the people who did amazing things to raise money, she ended up feeling useless.

To ease her conscience, she opened her bank account and contributed to a few worthy causes.

The days were beginning to blur into one long drawn out marathon of eating, sleeping, gazing through windows, watching flickering repeats on television, thinking and feeling helpless.

It seemed almost like a reward when the video call came in…

…But it wasn't her mother, it was the manager of the Care Home where Martha lived.

Accepting the call, she listened in stunned silence as the manager told her that her mother had been admitted to hospital, but she would not be able to visit her, or see her, probably, ever again.

He sat at his desk inside her monitor screen and cried as he told her what was happening and why. That the friend, with whom Martha watched quiz shows, was a new resident, sent by the local hospital for care – as a possible but untested Covid victim. Untested, because the tests were in short supply.

Silent, for a moment, he looked down at the paperwork in front of him and then, gathering courage, looked back at Lisa and continued.

He'd been informed by the hospital manager that "resources must be focussed on those who stood a chance of recovery. Old people are unlikely to recover, so treating them is a waste of time..." Following the conversation, the Care Home had received several new residents, sent from the hospital...

Lisa tried to absorb the words and failed, letting them wash over her as she stared at the man, sobbing, in front of her... what was his name? ...Brian?...

He told her how the care home had done its best to keep its residents and staff safe, that the new residents, sent from hospital, were meant to stay in isolation... but they were old... they didn't understand why they couldn't greet and embrace new friends, they didn't understand why they were at risk. They were unable to comprehend why the people they trusted had abandoned them to care homes, when they needed isolation and treatment.

Tears rolled down his face, splashing on the wooden surface of the desk, as he told her how his wife had cared for Martha, when her symptoms first developed, without the protective gear that the Home had been promised ...and how they had all improvised with old aprons and masks sewn late at night, following hastily written instructions from videos they'd found on the internet.

With his voice strained, he told her that Martha would not be alone, at the end, when it came to it, as his wife was with her, isolated and also critical. Choking, he listed the other residents to whom Martha had unwittingly passed the virus and, finally, he went silent. His swollen, sorrowful eyes watched her assimilate the horror and grief his news had brought, until she reached the same point of bewilderment and disbelief that he had been forced to face.

"We tried..." he said, "we tried. We did what we were asked to do and we cared – we could do no more – I am so sorry... ...and I'm sorry that I couldn't come to you , to tell you these terrible things, properly, somewhere where you could have a friend to console you and a shoulder to cry on... I had to tell my children, today, that they have to stay with their aunt, that they might never see their mother again – and that I will have to stay in the home with those of our residents who are still here ...until the end. That is the job I took on and it is the responsibility I must shoulder. I am just so sorry that we weren't..." He broke down, his body wracked with sobs and coughing, so she was unsure whether or not he finished his sentence.

What was she meant to say?

Thank you?

His wife had risked her life to help Martha and lost. He was clearly not far behind, but still trying to do his job, to help, to care. She loved her mother dearly, but could not believe, given the choice, that Martha would have wanted these unasked sacrifices made for her, even assuming she had any idea what was happening.

She might never see her mother again. Her mother would not understand – would be ill, fighting for her life and the only people around her were strangers.

Before she could speak to show him that she understood – that she was grateful for his family's care of her mother – for how much they'd tried to help – how sorry she was that they were paying a terrible price for caring for others, for taking risks that she would never have had the courage to do ...he ended the call.

That evening, when she saw her neighbours gathering in the street, in readiness for their accolade of thanks to the people who cared, nursed, doctored, delivered, protected and helped, she opened her window as wide as it would go, and banging a wooden spoon onto an old saucepan, she joined the cacophony of emotion – of fear and hope, of gratitude and community …and finally understood it.

Young Echoes

A stand-alone prequel short story for the
"Ghostly Echoes" Series

Mai Griffin

U P Publications

2019

Published as a free standalone taster for Mai Griffin's Ghostly Echoes Series – this story is not an extract from the books – it is a prequel to the first book "Ghostly Echoes" and is available on Kindle

Published by U P Publications

www.uppbooks.com
www.maiwriting.com
www.maigriffin.com

A Locked Vestry...

Mary and Prudence were in deep conversation at the far end of the church when Delia arrived. She sighed. Being new in the village, she had thought volunteering for flower arranging would be a good way to meet people, but mostly, it was just a sensible way to reduce the number of flowers in her pretty new garden.

Mary continued talking to Prudence and didn't even greet her as she walked by. She was pointing vaguely at some half-filled and empty vases, but Delia, upset by her rudeness, gritted her teeth; the woman had just assumed that she was here to work. On a table nearby, there was a bunch of dahlias and asparagus grass – even down to the colour – identical to those in her own garden; maybe there was a kindred spirit in the village after all...

She couldn't remember the last time that she'd had a decent conversation with anyone. The hospital visitor, who had sought to comfort her, lived here somewhere. She'd said her name was Sarah but without a surname she'd never find her. Her mother's arrival with Amanda had cut short Sarah's visit before she'd managed to get much past the pleasantries.

It was nice that, before she left, Sarah had

invited Delia to bring her daughter to play with Sarah's grandchild. Amanda was thrilled to hear that she and Emma were about the same age and danced around Sarah, her mother and grandmother, with glee.

Finding the atmosphere in the church to be chilly, in more ways than one, Delia decided that volunteering as a helper (with anything) could wait a little longer. Wandering outside in the fresh air, there was something else bothering her, but she couldn't remember what. She tried to recall what her mother said as she left – and why was she crying?

Prudence was so engrossed, listening to Mary's local gossip that she almost missed the little girl slipping into the church through the open door. That was odd, they hadn't left the door open. It was usually kept closed, between services, even when the "ladies who bloomed" (the vicar's pet name for his flower arrangers) were "blooming".

The child was about six years old – far too young to be running around on her own. Prudence watched to see where she went and waited for the child's parent or minder to appear at the door, looking for her.

The girl just plonked herself in the front row of the pews and sat there, quietly shaking. She looked upset.

When Prudence drew her attention to their small visitor, Mary stopped talking and marched straight down the aisle towards her, calling out as she strode "Hey! You, girl! What are you doing? Who are you? Where's your mother?"

The child was shivering with agitation and, as Mary neared, burst into loud wailing tears. Through the sobbing, Prudence and Mary heard her say something about her Mommy. She looked scared and with reason, Prudence thought; Mary, in her black witch-like dress, would look frightening to any small child.

Darting up from her seat, the girl yelled defiantly and ran to the nearest door. It was open and, before either lady could reach her, the child disappeared inside. The door banged shut and was bolted from within – the strident clang echoed throughout the almost empty church.

Sarah Grey and Polly, her friend and companion, were settling down to enjoy an hour of peace and quiet...

"You must be so sad, Sarah, that your husband never appears to you," Polly commiserated. "You see, and help, so many strangers in the world of spirit, it doesn't seem fair!"

Sarah smiled. "It really doesn't bother me. I sense Stephen with me most of the time and it's comforting. When my turn comes, we'll be together again, meanwhile, for as long as I can feel his warmth and know that he's here, it's enough." She eyed the tea trolley that Polly was pushing and was delighted to see that Polly had been baking again.

They'd known each other since Stephen had taken her to his home to meet his parents, months before they married. Polly had been the housekeeper there and, a few years older, had mollycoddled her from day one, making sure that her visits with Stephen were always a delight. Over the years they became close friends and after Stephen had died and Polly retired, they had set up house together.

Perhaps it was because they had been speaking of Stephen but, even so, it was strange that Sarah began to feel uneasy and she couldn't shake the feeling that she had to go to his graveside – not tomorrow or next week, but now!

Polly didn't question the sudden interruption of their quiet afternoon. "There has to be a good reason, Sarah. I'll get the car." On their arrival, Polly dropped Sarah at the Lychgate and went to park the car.

Still not quite believing how worried she felt, Sarah made her way to Stephen's graveside... Even before she reached it, she had the answer to her question. She saw Delia in the Church porch and recognized her as the seriously ill woman she had visited just over a week ago.

Seeing her so well – nothing like the one who had been at death's door, Sarah whispered *thank you Stephen* and hastened to speak to her. Something was wrong.

Seeing her, Delia was delighted but, before they could greet each other, they heard shouting and wails echoing inside the church and hurried to discover what was happening.

The Vicar had been called and, arriving the porch just as they approached, he quickly rushed ahead of Sarah, waving an apology for not stopping, but indicating that she should follow. Inside, they found that a dozen or so parishioners had joined the flower ladies – the scheduled bible meeting apparently forgotten. All had heard about the child in the vestry, but none had any idea of her identity.

The crowd parted, almost biblically, as the Vicar dashed up the aisle to the Vestry. Following closely behind him, Sarah and Delia made their way to the small, locked door. Delia noticed that although people made way for Sarah, greeting her as she passed, they still ignored her.

After hearing two agitated women trying to explain what had happened, Sarah stopped about a foot from the vestry door and stood, her head bowed, and eyes closed as if in prayer.

The small crowd stopped babbling and all human noise faded away as they waited for the drama to unfold. In the silence, Sarah could hear the girl's ragged breathing from behind the door.

Polly, who had now joined them, gestured to the vicar, warning him not to interrupt. Sarah very seldom initiated contact with the spirit world, but now, Polly guessed, she had no choice.

Intrigued, Delia joined Sarah and was surprised that nobody even glanced her way. Prudence and Mary continued to ignore her as did the rest of the crowd. The vicar didn't even acknowledge her when she walked right up to him, his eyes and full attention were riveted on Sarah standing near the Vestry door.

Unlike everyone else, Sarah smiled at her and said she was glad Delia had followed her.

Finally, someone with good manners! "What's going on?" she asked, "Why all the commotion? Everyone here is so rude, they won't talk to me, even when I tried to join in with flower-arranging"

"I think you know the little girl in the Vestry." Sarah smiled.

Delia looked blankly back "What girl?" she asked... Then she heard it ... the quiet sobbing from behind the door, asking for mummy... Amanda! What was Amanda doing here, she should be at school, today...?

Turning to the door, Sarah spoke.

"Hello Amanda. You are Amanda Spencer, aren't you?" The sobbing stopped and after a long pause, the child answered.

"Who are you?"

"I am Sarah, a friend of your mummy. I was with her when you visited the hospital."

"Where is she? Granny said they brought her here, but I can't find her. Do you know where my Mommy is?" Sarah smiled and the worried cleric looked relieved.

"When you come out, I have a message for you, from your mummy. She is worried about you, so please unlock the door."

Delia was indeed worried – she almost fainted, she so desperately wanted to comfort her child... Then her head cleared as if she had woken from deep sleep and she was inside the vestry with her arms around Amanda whispering soothing words to her, but Amanda could neither hear nor see her. It was only then that Delia understood, at last, what had happened to her. At least Amanda had stopped sobbing...

There was a loud click as the bolt slid back and, when Sarah indicated that they should, the vicar and Polly retreated a few yards.

From the shadows. They saw the child come out and within seconds, she was cradled in Sarah's arms listening to the comforting words her mother wanted to say to her.

When he heard Delia's name, the vicar recalled that only a few days ago he had officiated at the young woman's funeral, Delia Spencer.

As Polly drove her home, Amanda couldn't stop talking to the cleric who accompanied them. "Sarah said that my mommy is very sorry she had to leave me, but one day we really will be together again. She wants me to look after Grandma and Grandad and my baby brother so that Daddy can go to work without worrying about us ...and she said I must make sure my new puppy always has water in his dish."

Grandma met them at the door and took the child in her arms. "Wherever have you been Amanda? I was so worried, but thank goodness I had your call, Vicar, within minutes of arriving home." She thanked him and added, "I can't think what got into her! She knew I was going to the village and must have hidden in my car. Come in, come in, please. Tell me what happened"

Amanda went running to her baby brother, sleeping in his pram, and started to tidy the soft toys from around him. She seemed happy and had clearly found purpose in her new role as family protector.

Over tea, Sarah told them all about her conversation with Delia and explained that Delia had been so ill and confused, she hadn't even been aware that she had moved on. She remembered falling asleep in hospital, and didn't recall arriving home, but she'd felt fine and just carried on her life as normal.

She'd assumed that her husband had been

sparing her from family chores as she was still recovering. She spent most evenings walking, enjoying the balmy nights. Trevor always seemed to be asleep when she got home. If not, she assumed he was out at work. It hadn't felt odd.

As a newcomer in the small village, she was used to being ignored, but in the last few days, it had felt much worse than normal. Now, however, she understood. She was sad that she couldn't still be part of her family's life but was reassured when Sarah told her that she would be able to visit them whenever she liked.

It was unlikely that Amanda would be able to see her. Seeing close family was a rare talent, as Sarah knew. However, it was already clear that Amanda was responding to the love her presence brought. Delia was calmer, now, no longer angry and confused. It was hard to accept, but now she needed to adjust... Knowing that Sarah was there for her if ever she needed, was a great comfort.

By the time the vicar had been driven to his church and the car was garaged at home, Sarah was exhausted. Although the coffee was cold, the covered cakes and sandwiches had survived the wait, so Polly refreshed the percolator and they resumed what little was left of their day...

Also by Mai Griffin

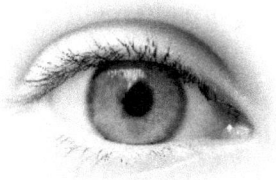 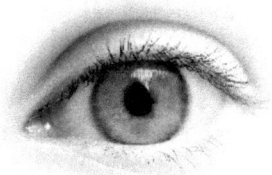

Thank you for reading Young Echoes, a short stand-alone taster about Sarah's frequently thwarted attempts to lead a normal life in the "Ghostly Echoes" series. To read more about Sarah's brushes with death, murder and the paranormal, the titles of Mai Griffin's full-length books follow...

Full length books
Ghostly Echoes Series
(Sarah and Polly)

Ghostly Echoes
A Poisonous Echo
Dangerous Echoes
Haunting Echoes
Restless Echoes

Stand Alone Fiction

Somebody Came

Short Stories

Picked and Mixed Anthology

Short Blasts

As an Illustrator

Donnington's Reef
Various publications for Dorchester Abbey, Oxon

For her paintings
www.maigriffin.com